"Your skin is amazing."

Brand's soap-slick hands glided across her shoulders and arms. "It's like one long pour of the thickest, richest cream, just waiting for me to lap you up."

He alternated soapy swirls with light tickles under her arms, across her breasts, and down her back, no inch of her skin escaping his attention. Then he gripped her bottom and locked her pelvis against his.

Paris linked her arms around his waist and closed her eyes as his strong thighs brushed hers. He was hard to her soft, rough to her smooth; every inch pure male.

UNTAMED

Untamed

Untamed

KATHLEEN LAWLESS

POCKET BOOKS
New York   London   Toronto   Sydney

POCKET BOOKS, a division of Simon & Schuster, Inc.
1230 Avenue of the Americas, New York, NY 10020

ISBN 0-7394-5916-3

Acknowledgments

Since writing is both solitary and a joint effort, there are many special people who deserve mention at this point in my career.

I'd like to thank my terrific agent, Maureen Walters, for her unflagging belief in me over the years.

What a joy and an honor to work with my wonderful editor, Micki Nuding, who understood from day one what I was about, and always encourages me to go for it. You are an author's dream.

To the art department at Pocket Books, who gives me the most magnificent covers. You rock!

To every single one of you, my readers, thank you for your enthusiastic letters and emails. You make sitting down to write each day a pleasure.

Special thanks are also due Reyna, for her inspiration and help in the creation of Forked Creek that day in the New York airport. Long may we shop!

Untamed

Chapter One

Her nose to the tour bus window, Paris waited impatiently for her first glimpse of Forked Creek, a restored ghost town and home to Martha May Brown's famous house of ill repute. She'd thought about little else ever since she first discovered Martha May's journal, now tucked safely into her compact travel bag.

"Hoo-eee! We are *so* not in Kansas anymore, Dorothy!" came a boisterous cry from the back of the bus.

Paris smiled in agreement. It had become the theme of the group's road trip from the Pacific Northwest into the Nevada desert.

She'd read that the ghost town was time-locked in its horse-and-buggy stage, which meant the modern-day roads necessary for emergency vehicles and tour buses ran discreetly behind the town, out of sight. When the bus finally rolled to a stop, Paris let the fifteen other women surge off ahead of her, leaving Paris free to approach the brothel once owned by her great-great-grandmother on her own.

The house looked pretty much the way she had envisioned, with its huge front porch and faded shingled exterior, sprawling three and a half stories high. She shaded her eyes against the Nevada sunshine as Hayley, the unofficial leader of the group, galloped up the front steps and banged loudly on the door. As the others followed, an attractive blonde in period costume stepped onto the porch.

"Welcome, ladies. My name is Valerie and I'll be your hostess during your visit to Forked Creek. Your rooms have been assigned and keys are ready for pickup inside. Are there any questions?"

"When do we get our costumes?"

Valerie smiled. "Everyone loves the costumes. Each of you has an extensive period wardrobe in your room, and you are strongly encouraged to remain 'in character' for your stay. Most visitors choose to do so, as it heightens the experience here."

There were nods and murmurs of assent from the group.

No problem, Paris thought. Having spent nearly thirty years molding herself into what she thought other people expected from her, the opportunity to be another person felt excitingly freeing.

As she collected her room key from Valerie, she said, "I can't wait to explore the town."

"There's plenty of time before dinner. Are you the librarian?"

Paris nodded. "How did you know?"

"A gal gets good at sizing people up quickly in this business. You're here doing historical research?"

"Yes." That was her cover, her reason for going off by herself every day.

"Feel free to ask as many questions as you like. I'm here to help," Val said.

"I'll be sure and take you up on that." Paris lifted her compact travel bag and made her way to her room on the second floor, conscious as she gripped the polished banister that this was the very house, the very town she'd been reading about ever since she found Martha May's journal last fall in her grandparents' attic.

The tag on her key ring read PANSY'S ROOM and as she walked down the hall she saw that each room was named after a woman. Martha May's working girls, she guessed, immortalized in this small way.

Pansy's was a corner room with windows on two sides; an armoire took up most of the far wall. The bed had an old iron frame and Paris mischievously wondered if Pansy used to handcuff her gentleman customers to it. A dressing screen occupied one corner near a washstand and basin. Framed needlepoint pictures dotted the walls, which were papered in large pink cabbage roses. Perhaps Pansy had filled her daytime hours with needlework.

What had Martha May's life been like here with no family, and no societal respectability? Had her great-great-grandmother been happy, or simply resigned to her life? She'd sounded happy in her journal entries, but she had also been on the cusp of change. Much like Paris. If things had turned out different, Paris would be a married woman today.

From the wardrobe she pulled out a nineteenth-century-style gown and held it against herself to view the effect in the cheval mirror, still hardly believing she was really here. Then, dress in hand, she crossed to the open window and leaned out. An ancient tree hugged the side of the house, and its leafy green foliage brushed her arm as she drank in the sight of the huge mountains guarding the town.

Somewhere out there a mine was located, not far from the hot springs, mentioned in the journal, and she could hardly wait to hit the trail of clues laid out in the book. Was it too far-fetched to hope that whatever treasure Martha May had hidden, more than a hundred years ago on her way out of town, was still waiting for her to uncover it?

Eager to explore, she went downstairs. On Main Street, she was amazed at how Forked Creek appeared untouched by time. What a labor of love the restoration must have been. She ran her hand along a scarred hitching post and envisioned her great-great-grandmother standing in this exact same spot, where raised wooden sidewalks fronted the line of shops with their freshly painted signs and horse-drawn wagons clip-clopped past at a leisurely pace.

Paris heard a shout from the far end of the street and saw

a crowd had gathered near the livery. She strolled down to join the onlookers outside a split-rail fence, then squeezed forward for a better view of the cowboy who stood inside the corral, a rope in his hand. At the other end of the rope, an extremely skittish-looking mare eyed him warily.

While most eyes were drawn to the horse, Paris's gaze was riveted on the man and the way all six-plus denim-clad feet of him exuded power and control. Nut brown leather chaps gloved his long, muscular legs and slapped together as he walked toward the horse. Did any garment better enhance a man's masculinity, the way they emphasized the exposed denim-V of his crotch?

Not that he required special clothing to prove that he was every inch a virile male. From fathomless dark eyes beneath winged brows, a square jaw peppered with a day's growth of whiskers, and capable broad shoulders tapering to lean hips, everything about him proclaimed him pure alpha male.

Paris sighed as she leaned against the fence and watched him. When he removed his leather gloves and tucked them into his back pocket, her sigh deepened, for he had fabulous hands, big and strong. And judging by the way he handled the horse he certainly knew how to use them. She couldn't pull her gaze from those large, tanned, masculine hands stroking the horse's silky neck.

What would those hands feel like caressing her—sliding slowly up over her hips and waist to finally cup her breasts, as his dark smoldering eyes gazed into hers with desire?

Her nipples tightened. He'd slowly unbutton her blouse, drawing out the anticipation one button at a time, finally unveiling her lacy bra. Beads of perspiration dewed her hairline, and her breathing grew shallow.

The horse tossed her head and rolled her eyes at the cowboy, letting him know he wasn't going to have his way with her. Not yet. Undaunted, the cowboy continued his soothing caress, and Paris shivered as his gaze met hers.

Paris flushed, unable to look away. It was almost as if he could read her thoughts, know her desire. The possibility aroused her further, making the blood pound in her veins. After a long breathless moment, he turned his attention back to the horse.

The crowd cheered as he reeled the mare close and flung a saddle on her back. The horse pranced a little, as if she had won the contest, and Paris wondered if the cowboy always singled out someone in the audience to play to.

Suddenly feeling in need of a cold drink, Paris headed back down Main Street.

The saloon doors swung open on silent hinges and her footsteps rang against the wooden floor as she crossed the room. She leaned against the gleaming mahogany bar and hooked her foot on the brass railing, examining the gleaming liquor bottles lining the shelves behind the bar. Close at hand were heavy brass beer taps.

"What'll you have?" asked the burly bartender.

"Just a club soda."

A deep masculine voice drawled from the doorway, "Tearoom's at the other end of town."

Paris slowly turned toward the speaker silhouetted in the doorway. His face was shadowed beneath a black Stetson, and a faded denim jacket clung to his wide shoulders. As he started toward her, brown leather chaps shifted on his hips, emphasizing the triangle of denim sheathing his masculine attributes.

Her cowboy.

He advanced with a jangle of spurs and the solid tread of well-worn boot heels. Up close he was even more ruggedly good-looking, and his dark eyes hinted at something untamed about their owner. Right now those eyes were frankly bar-coding her.

His gaze moved from her eyes to her lips, then dropped to linger on the shadowy cleavage revealed by the scooped neckline of her costume.

His X-ray vision breached the exotic lingerie she secretly indulged in and devoured her beneath the clothes. Paris had never felt so achingly, meltingly female as heat tingled from her breasts to her belly.

"You're not going to make me drink alone, are you? You look like a chardonnay kind of girl," he drawled. "Doesn't she, Hank?"

"Actually, I prefer sauvignon blanc," she said coolly.

A half-filled wineglass instantly appeared before her, next to a tumbler of whiskey. His eyes locked to hers, the cowboy clinked his whiskey glass against her wineglass and swallowed. Her gaze followed the long, tanned line of his throat as he drank. They sure didn't grow men like this in Seattle.

As Paris took a sip of her wine, the cowboy rested his elbows on the bar. "New to Forked Creek?"

"Yes. No. Not really." She'd been reading about this place

and envisioning it for months now. Even tried to phone the mayor.

He cocked a brow. "You sure?"

She cleared her throat. "My great-great-grandmother used to live here."

"Really?" he asked, tossing back his drink. "What was her name?"

"Martha May Brown. She ran the brothel, and wrote about it in her journal."

"So here you are, set to visit the scene of her misadventures?"

Paris smiled secretively. "Something like that."

"Come on then. I'll show you around." He set his empty glass down on the gleaming bar where it was whisked away by the ever-efficient Hank, who had been eavesdropping unabashedly. "What's your name, Princess?"

Princess? She rolled her eyes, but couldn't deny his charm.

"Paris. Paris Sommer."

"Mitchell Brand the third. Folks call me Brand." His tone told her he was proud of his name, proud of who he was. "Well, Paris Sommer, you're in Forked Creek now. The normal rules don't apply." He took her hand and warmth tingled through her again.

"Which normal rules?"

"Ones like 'don't talk to strangers.' We're all strangers here, our lives intersecting for a brief moment in time. Take advantage of it and run with it."

There were other things she'd like to take advantage of

and run with. "Are you sure it's no trouble?" Paris felt a quiver of excitement. Was it the old-fashioned clothing, the freedom of pretending to be someone else, or the sheer magnetism of the man beside her that had her feeling flustered and fluttery, unlike her usual calm and cool self?

Mitchell Brand flung his arm around her shoulder. "Darlin', I have the distinct feeling you're going to be a whole lot of trouble."

Suddenly his cell phone rang, sounding totally out of place and effectively breaking the mood.

"Brand here. Right now? Yeah."

He snapped the phone shut. "Afraid our little tour will have to wait for another time."

Paris nodded and swallowed her disappointment as she watched him leave the saloon. Men like Mitchell Brand never spent much time with her. She'd learned that the hard way not long ago.

BRAND RESENTED BEING summoned like a schoolkid to the principal's office—which in his case had been the commander's office of the military college, where he'd always seemed to be on report.

Warren West, great-grandson of the town's founder, had gotten himself elected town mayor, and his office was the largest one in the town hall. With no computers or modern amenities, it was more of a stage than a functioning office, a place for Brand's stepbrother to hold court.

Warren looked pissed. "I told you I require regular updates."

"And I told you, when there's something you need to be informed about, you will be. I've only been here three days."

"Time's running out, Brand. I need you to find that deed, not get distracted by every pretty tourist who comes to town." So the bartender was a snitch. Figured. "This one's different," Brand said. "I need you to check her out. Paris Sommer. Claims to be kin of Martha May."

"She's here?"

"You know her?"

"She called my office sometime last year. I thought she was a crank-caller. If she came all this way, she must know something."

It was pathetic to see the way Warren perked right up, like a dog thrown a bone. He never would have made it in the Special Services. Still, Brand felt a twinge of sympathy for the other man. Warren's destiny had been decided before his birth, his legacy being this town and the preservation of its "authenticity." The company started by his grandfather and carried on by his father had gone public, making Warren more of a puppet of the shareholders than an authority figure. He wasn't the one who wielded the scepter of authority in the West clan.

Warren wet his lips in a nervous-excited habit Brand recalled from their youth. "Stick with her. I'll see what I can find out. If she's for real, maybe she can lead us to the deed."

"Sticking with her was precisely what I was up to when I was interrupted by your call," Brand pointed out.

"I needed to make sure you were still on the job."

Brand leaned across Warren's desk, his face level with the other man's, well aware of the way Warren shrank back from him. "I'm here because you claim I owe you—no other reason. And when I'm done, we're done. That clear?"

Behind them came a loud rapping on the open office door. Brand swung about to see a heavyset, middle-aged man paste a phony grin across his jowly mug.

"Luke." Warren stood behind his desk and extended his hand to the older man. Brand raised his brow in a silent question, which Warren ignored.

The old boy brushed past Brand as if he were invisible. "A little birdie's been chirping in my ear, Warren. Saying maybe you're not telling me everything you know."

"What makes you think Warren knows anything?" Brand asked.

Beetled brows knitted together as the older man slowly turned and took Brand's measure. "The prodigal stepbrother, I assume. It appears Warren knows enough to call you."

Brand chose to deliberately misinterpret the other man's words. "Why did you call me down here, Warren?"

"Thought it was high time for you to meet Luke Lamoy."

"I keep telling the boy here that we're well on our way to being partners. He doesn't always seem to take me serious," Lamoy told Brand.

Brand waited to see what Warren would say, Warren, true to form, didn't say a word. He'd always been that way, preferring to say nothing rather than risk saying the wrong thing. And it was hardly Brand's place to step in. Maybe the silence was effective, for eventually the visitor hitched his belt beneath his middle-aged girth and headed for the door.

"I'm off then, if there's nothing I need to be filled in on. I'd best say howdy to that daughter of mine before she gets wind that I'm in town and haven't seen her yet. Give my best to your mother, Warren. Always did think of you two as family." The door slammed behind Luke and Warren dropped back into his chair.

"You know what Lamoy wants, don't you?" Warren asked.

"I'm betting it's something to do with that deed you're so fired up about."

"It'll be a major toehold in the town for him if he can pull it off."

"Is it worth the fight?"

"I have a responsibility to this place, these people. The shareholders. I'm sure that's hard for you to grasp, since responsibility never seemed big in your vocabulary."

Brand shook his head. "You don't know me at all. No one does." He left the office without a backward glance, wishing he were anyplace other than Forked Creek.

PARIS FELT LIKE SHE NEEDED to pinch herself, to remind herself she was really, truly here. The Wild West ghost town was run almost like a theme park; everyone was encouraged to playact the past. Families on vacation walked by dressed in period costume, wide-eyed with amazement.

A stagecoach rolled past her and pulled to a stop near the hotel. The coach's door opened and out stepped a woman and a little boy, followed by two rough-looking men dressed head to toe in black, guns strapped to their thighs. Everywhere she looked, it was like a minidrama.

A peek in the barbershop window showed a man being shaved with a straight razor. The saloon doors flew open and a man landed face-first in the street. He picked himself up, let out a roar, and charged back inside.

Paris crossed the street to window-shop at the milliner's, where she found herself drawn to a cherry red hat complete with a veil and a silver fan-shaped hat pin. Martha May might have hankered after a hat like this.

As she headed back to the bordello the town clock struck five. Now that she had an idea of the layout of the town, she hoped Martha May's map would make better sense.

Inside the house, she paused at the foot of the stairs, hearing raised voices. ". . . didn't raise you to spend your days playacting," a man said.

Val's voice replied, "You didn't raise me at all."

"I raised you to respect your elders, and that's a fact."

"Since when did respect include pimping . . ."

The rest of Val's response was too muffled to be heard. The door opened and a burly middle-aged man stepped out, his scowl changing to a wide smile as he caught sight of Paris.

"Well, hello there, little lady. Y'all must be new in town."

"Why, yes I am." She didn't trust this man; he was too fake. Fake tan, fake-white teeth, fake smile. She took half a step back even as he extended his right hand.

"Luke Lamoy, Valerie's father."

"Paris Sommer." Her hand was swallowed by his beefy one.

"Miss Sommer. I expect you'll find yourself feeling right at home."

Moments later Val appeared, looking unsettled. Paris noticed she didn't make eye contact. Was she afraid of her own father?

"Hello, Paris. Are you returning or leaving?"

"I've been exploring the town."

"How energetic of you. Most of the girls are napping till supper. Would you like water for a bath?"

"I don't suppose there's a shower."

"No, there's no shower here. Only over at the hotel."

"A bath would be lovely."

"I'll send the water right up. Supper is promptly at six. How do you like Forked Creek so far?"

"Very interesting. I met someone who offered to show me around."

Val stiffened. "Really. Was it Warren West by any chance? He's the mayor. Old-time family from these parts."

"No, I haven't met him, but I sure would like to." Part of Paris wanted to mention Mitchell Brand and see what Val knew about him, but she picked up an odd vibe that kept her silent.

Dinner was a lively boardinghouse-style affair, after which the women retired to their rooms to dress for the evening ahead and whatever escapades that might bring. Paris was anxious to begin her treasure hunt, but didn't want to call attention to herself with such an early absence. She was looking through the closet for something to wear when Hayley blew into her room and flopped onto her bed. Clad in a white cotton eyelet camisole with matching bloomers, she looked like someone from a Western movie set.

"Isn't this a hoot? Like Disneyland for grown-ups."

"It's great," Paris agreed.

"And a real, honest-to-goodness bordello." Hayley dropped her voice to low and conspiratorial. "There's talk."

"What kind of talk?"

"About men. Gorgeous young men. Serviceable young men."

Paris grinned. "Now that I find difficult to believe."

"Spoil sport." Hayley lobbed a pillow in her direction. "Can't a girl hope?"

Paris laughed and selected an evening dress. She loved the way the costumes made it easy to slide into someone else's skin. She was no longer Paris Sommer, raised by strict elderly grandparents. She was a freewheeling, fun-loving gal from Forked Creek. That was much simpler than wrestling with who she really was: the good-girl granddaughter . . . the conscientious employee . . . or the recently jilted bride. Or something else?

Hayley left to get dressed and Paris soon headed downstairs to the parlor, following the sounds of music and female chatter. A pianist belted out a muted honky-tonk tune in the corner while the women drank and laughed and played cards. Then the parlor door opened to admit a group of men, and the energy in the room changed. The women flirted and played up to the men, sitting on their laps and loosening their ties.

The retreat was advertised as a place where anything

could and did happen. Would some of the women take their gentlemen upstairs? And if they did, would the games end at the doorway . . . or lead to something else?

The door opened a second time to silhouette a man's figure, and Paris's breath caught.

Her cowboy.

As his eyes met hers across the room, the piano music and chatter faded away. All she could hear was a sudden rushing in her ears, a singing in her blood, as he crossed the room to her side.

"I guessed this is where I'd find you."

Paris smiled. "At the scene of Martha May's misadventures?"

His lips quirked in a half smile. "Exactly. So how about asking me up to your room?"

Chapter Two

"*My room? Why?*" Paris tried to keep her voice even, though her pulse leaped with anticipation.

He leaned in close, his words for her ears alone. "Trust me—that's the way the game is played here."

What would the others think if she went upstairs alone with him? Paris glanced around the room. Had some of them already left with a man?

"What's the matter—not feeling comfortable as a soiled dove?" Brand teased.

"More like not feeling comfortable with you," Paris blurted.

"Smart woman. We should get along." His hand on the small of her back nudged her across the room, the heat of his touch seared her skin through her thin silk gown. He was aptly named; she felt branded.

Had the temperature in the room gone up, or was it just the warmth of his hand, the way his eyes singled her out? Paris was way out of her league, but she'd sooner die than reveal that, so she nonchalantly led the way up the staircase to her room as if it happened every day.

Once inside, he sprawled across her bed as if no stranger to her or their surroundings. "It gets cool in the evenings. I'd suggest you change into something warmer."

"Where are we going?"

"I heard you're a librarian, in town doing historical research. Thought you might be interested in the cemetery."

Paris shot him a sharp look. She loved old cemeteries, and the one in Forked Creek was high on her list of must-sees. How had he known that? When he showed no signs of moving, she selected a warm-looking long-sleeved dress and stepped behind the corner screen to change.

The second she was out of sight, Brand dove for her unpacked overnight bag. When he unzipped it, bright, frothy silk met his eyes. Hmm . . . the lady liked her lingerie. He dug through layers of lacy nothings, growing aroused as he imagined her in them. The old-time clothing she was wearing displayed her hourglass figure perfectly, and he'd bet she didn't need a corset for shaping. Not that stays and corsets weren't a whole lot of fun. He began to harden at the thought of unlacing her corset, and reminded himself to keep his mind on the business at hand—even if it did include Paris Sommer, her tawny hair streaked with gold as if kissed by the sun, a fall of liquid silk brushing her shoulders.

She gave an outraged cry behind him, and the faded book he'd just found beneath her underwear slipped through his fingers. *Busted!*

"Just what do you think you're doing?"

He grabbed hold of the first solid thing in her bag—a box of condoms—gratified to see her flush of embarrassment. "Making sure that you're prepared. Glad to see that you are."

Paris knew she was blushing bright red as she faced him. Damn Janine! Her best friend had slipped the condoms into Paris's bag when she wasn't looking, along with some other items she'd prefer her nosy visitor not find, including chocolate body paint.

"I should have known you weren't to be trusted." She reached his side and tugged on the bag's strap.

He held firm with one hand, and continued to delve with the other. "I don't suppose this is really a tube of lipstick?"

"Give me that!" The bag dropped to the floor between them.

"What, this?" He was clearly enjoying himself far too much as he pulled off the top of the tube and gave the base a deft twist. The plastic toy started to vibrate against his palm.

"Let me guess. This is to help cure a headache." He touched the vibrating lipstick-shaped plastic tip to her temple, then slowly drew it down the side of her face, across her neck and her chest, pausing just above the neckline of her low-cut dress.

Paris trembled, hot, then cold. He was far more potent stimulation than anything that ran on batteries.

"It's not what you think," she squeaked. "My girlfriend thought . . ."

"That you'd benefit from the attentions of a battery-operated boyfriend? Less mess than the real thing?" His finger followed the path the vibrator had taken, then dipped teasingly inside the neckline of her gown to stroke along her cleavage, making Paris all too aware that he was the bona-fide "real thing," whom she desired with a primitive intensity that shocked her. She wanted to wallow in the raw sexuality that oozed from his every pore. As she swayed toward him, he suddenly withdrew his finger.

"Let's go," he said briskly.

She blinked. Apparently, despite the deep and smoldering looks, he didn't feel the same sexual attraction she did.

OUTSIDE, DARKNESS HAD FALLEN, softening the definition between town and surrounding hills, which added to the air of unreality. Paris shivered slightly in anticipation. A heartbeat later Brand's jacket settled across her shoulders, warm and scented with his masculine outdoor smell.

"This way." He steered her around back, where a large horse was tied to a hitching post. "Horses were always out back of the bordello so that no one passing by would know who was inside," he said. "Do you ride?"

"No." Paris shook her head. Seen up close, that was one huge animal.

"There's a first time for everything." He positioned her

foot into the stirrup and hefted her into the saddle before she knew what was happening. Her long skirt was clearly not designed for riding astride; it rode up indecently high on her thighs, while her thong underwear was a scant barrier between her and the leather saddle. Brand swung into place behind her and reached around for the reins, his forearm gently brushing her breast.

Her body's response was so hard and swift, she almost gasped. Her nipples were tight and aching, sending tremors of desire low in her belly. He settled himself behind her, his jeans-clad legs snugged against her exposed thighs, making her aware of how suggestively her bare legs were spread across the saddle. Her mons was pressed against the curve of the saddle horn while her tush was cradled against his maleness, and as the horse started to move the saddle rubbed intimately against her, swamping her with sexual desire. She bit back a moan. It had been far too long since she'd last had sex, if a saddle was turning her on!

The bordello was situated on one end of town, and the church cemetery was located on the other end. The church stood on a slight rise as if watching over the townsfolk, a visual reminder to keep the congregation in line the other six days of the week.

They circled around the church to the back, where the land continued to slope upward, then leveled out. Wispy clouds crossed the nearly full moon to reveal shadowy headstones and crosses. In the distance, Paris heard the roll of thunder.

"Is that a light up ahead?"

Brand swore and dug his heels into the horse's flanks, urging their mount forward faster. Paris clutched the saddle horn and hung on as they crossed the uneven ground up to the cemetery.

Ahead, she heard a muffled shout and saw a lantern extinguished. By the time they reached the spot the intruders were long gone, but signs of their efforts remained.

"Damn grave robbers," Brand said. "People think they can dig up the past and maybe find something of value."

"Looks like we got here in time," Paris said. A small pile of dirt was displaced but no coffin was yet in sight.

Behind her, she heard Brand on his cell phone reporting the incident. "Nope, didn't manage to get a clear look. Dressed in dark clothing. Otis. Not sure if it was a random pick or not. Yeah, do that." He flipped the phone shut.

"You know whose grave this is?"

He was silent a moment as if deciding how much to tell her. "Otis Lam was the founder and original owner of nearly all of Forked Creek. He was also a good friend of Martha May's."

Paris opened her mouth to exclaim "Otis from the journal" then closed it again abruptly. "So it may or may not be coincidental that they picked this grave."

"Security's on it." His arms tightened around her as he turned the horse around.

"Where are we going?"

"Back. We're going to try to beat the rain."

The ominous rumble of thunder had grown noticeably closer. Before they went much farther the skies opened up, soaking them to the skin in less than a minute.

Lightning cracked and the horse bolted, but Brand immediately regained control and directed it toward the livery.

Inside the building, he dismounted in one easy movement. Paris swung her leg over the saddle and slid what seemed a very long way to the ground. She landed with a thud against Brand, who caught her. She could feel his hard strength at every juncture of their bodies, and a most masculine stirring from one part in particular.

She glanced up at him, making no move to step away.

He cleared his throat. "You know, looking at a man the way you're looking at me is a surefire way to get yourself into trouble."

Paris leaned into him slightly. If he was the flame, she was about to get well and truly burned. "Are you trouble, Brand?" she asked huskily.

"Princess, I am more trouble than you could ever imagine."

She stared up at him, slowly moistening her lips. His mouth lowered to capture hers, and his legs nudged hers apart to press hard against the throbbing ache at the juncture of her thighs. As he greedily plundered her mouth, his knuckles brushed her nipples, sending a jolt of electricity straight to her core. Her underwear was damp, moistened by the dew of her desire, and she stretched up on her toes, intensifying the friction of his hard cock against her inflamed wellspring of sensation.

He finally dragged his mouth from hers, and pulled away from her, catching his breath as he fought for control. He stared down at her with raw desire, and excitement spiraled through her.

"Princess, kiss a man like that and you're bound to find yourself in danger."

Already missing his heat, Paris wrapped her arms around her middle. "I can take care of myself."

Brand doubted it. What the hell had possessed him to kiss her? Other than the way she'd been looking at him, like she'd never seen a man before and suddenly realized what she'd been missing. She kissed the same way, and he'd bet she'd make love that way, too. As if it was the first time and the last time all in one. Which was exactly the way Brand liked it: One-night stands meant no complex emotions.

His body still reacted to the faintly musky smell of her, which annoyed him. While he'd heard about pheromones, he'd never found himself spellbound in their grip before. Abruptly he turned and hefted the saddle off the back of Quicksilver.

"Can I help?"

He gave her a long, level look, taking the time to notice the way she filled out her wet dress in all the right places.

"Know anything about horses?"

She shook her head, setting that silky curtain of hair in motion.

"Then I suggest you stay out of the way."

She pressed her full lips together. It was a librarian's look, no doubt reserved for pesky patrons who dared speak above a whisper in her hallowed halls.

"Is there a towel so I can dry off?"

"I like you wet."

She caught her breath. It had been an outrageous thing to say, dripping with double entendre.

She faced him, arms akimbo. "Why? So I'm vulnerable?"

He stepped toward her with a swagger, expecting her to step back, secretly pleased when she didn't—not even when two long strides turned into three and brought him flush up against her.

"Princess, you have no idea just how truly vulnerable you are."

"And you're just the man to show me, I suppose?"

If he thought he could scare her off with he-man tactics, he was in for a surprise.

He grinned. "Let's get out of here." He headed toward the livery door.

Rain had transformed the wheel ruts in the road into rivers. Paris shivered as a gust of wind lashed them with droplets of freezing rain.

"Ready to make a run for it?"

Before she could answer, he ran across Main Street, pulling her with him as he steered clear of the biggest puddles. They burst into the dimly lit lobby of the hotel, where a nineteenth-century-looking gentleman sat behind the desk.

"Evening, Mr. Brand." He handed over a key, taking little notice of Paris or her bedraggled state. Perhaps he was accustomed to seeing Brand with different women.

She straightened her shoulders. No way would she be one of a posse.

"Evening, William. It's a wet one out there."

"Yes, sir."

The stairs and banister were made of a rich dark wood set off by a red floral runner. Brand turned left at the end of the hall, with Paris at his side. She, who'd never been a risk-taker, was about to follow a man she'd just met into his hotel room. Who had she turned into, and what had happened to her normal, cautious self?

Brand unlocked the door, then ushered her inside. What on earth she was doing?

"What now?"

He advanced toward her. "Oh, I'm sure we'll think of something."

Paris nervously shifted her gaze from him to the room, so rich in historical detail it looked like a museum. The large and comfy-looking sleigh bed was puffed high with a feather duvet. Excitement shivered through her as she sat on a crushed-velvet settee near the fire and stretched her hands to its warmth.

"You're cold," Brand said with a frown, as he touched her icy shoulder.

"I'm soaked to the skin. And it's not like there's central heating."

"Go warm up in the shower. There's a clean robe on the back of the door."

The curl of excitement intensified. Alone with Brand, clad only in a robe? Did she dare? She stood, determined to go for it. Besides, refusing and risking a chill seemed foolish.

"Thanks, I don't mind if I do."

The bathroom's tile floor was heated, she discovered

when she pulled off her boots and curled her cold, wet feet against it.

After she'd stripped off her wet things she gave herself an assessing glance in the full-length mirror. Not bad for pushing thirty. Not perfect, but nothing to be ashamed of, either. Certainly no one who deserved to be jilted in front of everyone she knew. She was better off without Joel, and lucky she had discovered it before rather than after. Still, a little romp with her cowboy might be just the salve she needed for her wounded pride.

She stepped into the steam-filled shower stall, raised her head, and let the hot water pummel her face and neck and shoulders. It had to be a massage-pulse showerhead, for the fingers of spray were total sensuality. Her nipples had hardened as if being grazed by a lover's caress. She cupped her breasts in her palms and raised them to more fully receive the darting tongulike attention of the water jets, rewarded by a sweet tightening sensation between her legs.

She turned and felt the shower spray lash her shoulders, and moved forward to let the fingers of water massage her buttocks. Her entire body throbbed and pulsed deliciously.

She turned again to face the showerhead, hands against the sleek tile walls, legs slightly apart, trying to soothe the growing ache in her loins. She closed her eyes, imagining Mitchell Brand, wet and naked, rubbing himself against her and . . .

"Oh!" She whirled. He was there! As naked and virile as she had only dared imagine.

His jaw brushed the sensitive ridge of her shoulder as he

spoke softly in her ear. "I'll wash your back if you wash mine." He rubbed himself slowly and sensually against her, breast to chest, pelvis to pelvis, thigh to thigh.

Paris melted against him in a wordless, timeless dance, the shower spray their accompanying music, the heavy pounding of her heart supplying the rhythm. Brand's hands explored every plane and valley, crevice and curve, while she savored his sleek musculature.

His dampened chest hair stimulated her sensitive nipples in the most divine torture; his cock arrowed toward her, primed and ready. She reached for it, only to have him step back.

Brand dropped to his knees before her and gently widened her stance to allow him access to her womanly secrets. Paris braced herself with her hands against the wall. At the first brush of his fingertips against her supersensitized labia, she tensed, then gasped in delight when talented lips and tongue replaced his fingers.

She felt her female petals swell and blossom in welcome. A radiant pleasure lapped through her—slowly at first, then gathering momentum as he traced the delicate shape of her inner lips. Her insides continued to heat as his lips nuzzled and his tongue darted in and out, playing hide-and-seek with her hidden pearl. Wave after wave of divinely intense sensation saturated her as she drank in the sight of his sleek dark head between her legs, and savored the magic of his tongue. Her breath caught, then caught again in a soft gasp as, finally, blessed release consumed her.

Brand didn't stop there, but continued to lick and lap

and tease her to new torturous heights. Paris responded like a wild woman, her hips gyrating with his moves. Slowly, then faster, then slowing back down again, she experienced it all. Aftershocks rippled through her and crested into new orgasmic waves of pleasure until Paris had no idea where one orgasm left off and the next one began. Her body achieved things she never would have believed possible, and she was throbbing and limp and thoroughly sated when Brand finally rose.

He kissed her hard and she tasted herself on his lips, musky and salty-sweet. She could barely stand. The shower jets continued their caress while Brand teased her nipples to new pinnacles of delight as his hot turgid cock nuzzled her outer lips, then lightly brushed her swollen bud.

Swamped in sensation, she moaned, wanting more!

He lifted her hands and wrapped them around the neck of the showerhead for support, then boosted her up till her legs were wrapped around his hips, his hard cock inches from penetration.

Chapter Three

Paris looked down at Brand's throbbing erection and moaned as his velvet tip nuzzled her, rubbing her inside and out. She squirmed to bring him fully inside her, to fill her throbbing emptiness with him, and whimpered when his large hands held her still.

"You like that?"

Wordlessly, she nodded.

"You want more?"

She nodded more vigorously.

"Say it. 'I want you, Brand.'"

"I want you, Brand. *In* me."

"Deep."

"And hard! Would you *please* just put it in?" she implored, as he continued, inflaming every over-sensitized nerve ending to a fever pitch.

"Princess, I intend to give you the wildest ride you've ever had."

He rolled on a condom and when Paris finally felt the pressure of his slow, sure entry she moaned with delight.

He leaned forward and sipped her lips, swallowing her sounds of pleasure. He gave a low growl of his own as she tightened her inner muscles and pivoted her hips to accommodate him more fully. She felt his throbbing length fill her completely, then he started to withdraw. She instinctively tightened everything to prevent his retreat, but before she had time to register the emptiness he was back, doubling and redoubling his pace, increasing the friction as he filled and re-filled her.

She watched his cock slide rhythmically in and out, the pummeling of the shower heightening the intensity of their joining. It was so intense, so frenzied, so sublime, it was impossible to tell where he ended and she began. Paris turned her face into her arm to muffle her scream as the most intense orgasm of her life splintered into slivers of sensation that rippled through every particle of her.

Brand halted abruptly, fighting for control of his breathing.

"What?" Paris asked anxiously. "Is something wrong?"

"Hell, no. Too right." Slowly, deliberately he resumed his movements.

Paris relaxed and simply enjoyed the feel of him sliding slowly, divinely in and out of her.

"I could do this forever," she murmured.

"I wish I could say the same thing."

"What?" Paris teased. "No self-control?"

"Enough." Brand smiled. "I'm not going to come until you do at least once more."

She laughed. "I couldn't possibly."

"We'll just see about that."

He grasped her buttocks and shifted the angle of his entry and Paris's eyes widened at the new sensations. "Oh my!"

"Good?"

"Too good."

"It's never too good."

He reached between them and found the tiny pearl of her swollen clitoris. Gently he thumbed it in an ever-widening circular motion. Pressure built as he rubbed her, keeping rhythm with his cock moving in and out of her, faster and faster. Paris spun out of control, and at the crescendo of her climax she felt Brand tense, then heard his hoarse cry of triumphant release.

She leaned forward and wrapped her arms around him, resting her head on the broad strength of his shoulder.

She nibbled at the knotted cord in his neck, licking the droplets of water from his skin. She could feel the heavy thud of his heart against her breast and ran her fingers through his damp tangle of chest hair, loving its coarse, soft texture. Paris flung her head back and let the shower rain upon her face. She felt amazing, light, carefree, and fully sated.

"Think you can stand?" Brand carefully set her back down on her feet and continued to caress her. "Your skin is amazing," he said as his soap-slick hands glided across her shoulders and arms. "It's like one long pour of the thickest, richest cream, just waiting for me to lap you up."

He alternated soapy swirls with light tickles under her arms, across her breasts, and over her buttocks, no inch of her skin escaping his attentions. His touch naturally succeeded in arousing her, particularly when he gripped her buttocks and locked her pelvis against his.

She linked her arms around his waist, closed her eyes, and gave herself over to their timeless dance. His strong, hair-roughened thighs brushed hers, a sensation she savored to the fullest. He was hard to her soft, rough to her smooth, every inch pure male. She gripped his backside, treated it to long, loving strokes, and felt an immediate stirring from his cock. Her sated insides responded with sweet, damp heat that weakened her knees and made her melt against him.

He tilted her chin up and she opened her eyes to his intense dark gaze. "Feel what you do to me?"

"Mmmmmmmm." Speech was far too much effort. Best save her energy for more important things, like kissing. She leaned forward and helped herself, savoring the feel of his lips on hers as their mouths shaped and reshaped one another's till they found the perfect fit.

The woman kissed like an angel, Brand thought. Luckily there was nothing angelic about her body's fevered response to his, the way she held nothing back. That could prove dangerous; a person always ought to hold something in reserve.

She sank to her knees before him, grasped his buttocks and began to lick his cock—slowly at first, as if she weren't sure of herself, then with growing enthusiasm as he rose to the occasion. Her tongue snaked his length from base to tip, following the sensitive seam on the underside before she swirled the tip in a move that drove him mad. Rather than attempt to swallow him whole, she continued her dainty, ladylike exploration. With just the tip of him fully inside her mouth, she grasped him midstaff and made a ring with her thumb and forefinger to pump him hard while she sucked.

"Whoa!" Brand pulled back before the game was over way too soon. "Too good." He barely recognized the guttural sound of his own voice.

"Excellent." She had found the soap and now massaged his balls with soap-slippery fingers before she found that special sweet spot between his cock and his balls.

"Princess. Paris." He pulled her back up before she could realize just how much she had tested his self-control. "You're turning the tables on me, darlin'."

"How's that?" she murmured as she nibbled at the corners of his mouth, sharing his taste on her lips. He sipped, already addicted to her. Her smell. Her taste. The feel of her soft wet skin on his.

"I think we're starting to shrivel that beautiful skin of yours. What say we adjourn to the other room?"

She pressed her luscious lips together, pretending to consider. "I suppose we could."

He reached behind her and shut off the water.

"I've never made love in the shower before," she said. "I like it."

"We'll have to see what else we can do to broaden that neglected education of yours." As he spoke he draped a warm fluffy towel across her shoulders.

"Heated towels?"

"The towel bars are heated with hot water, same as the floors. Otis, who originally built this place, spared no expense." Brand dried himself with swift, economical movements and shrugged into one of the robes on the back of the door, then passed the second robe to Paris.

She knotted its belt around her waist, having twisted her hair up into one of those turban things that women did. He gave his hair a swift rub with the towel, then pushed it back out of his eyes.

"I'm afraid there's no hair dryer," he said. "But the gas fire's on." Paris needed no second invitation to plop herself before the fireplace in the other room to dry her hair.

Over the sound of running water, she heard his cell phone beep from the bedside table and she rose to pick it up, intending to take it in to him. A text message scrolled across the screen and her own name leaped out at her: PARIS SOMMER LEGIT. KEEP AN EYE ON HER.

Paris's entire body went stiff and she dropped the phone back onto the table as if it had stung her.

Should she confront him with what she'd just learned? Or put on her soaking dress and return to the brothel?

She flung open the wardrobe door but as she suspected, it contained only men's clothing. As she was considering her options, she heard a discreet knock on the suite door. Warily she opened it a crack and looked out. A black-suited man handed her her overnight bag.

"Sorry to bother you, miss, but Mr. Brand requested I fetch this for you from Miss Valerie's."

"Thank you." She shut the door and checked to ensure the journal was safe, then buried it way back down at the bottom.

Brand strolled casually out of the bathroom. "Oh good. Your bag got here."

"How dare you?" Paris demanded.

He took a half step backward, hands in the air as if she had leveled a gun at him. "Maybe it was a little high-handed, but I figured there would be stuff in there you wanted after your shower."

"You make a habit of this?" Paris asked. "Full service for Forked Creek visitors? No wonder it's such a popular destination."

His eyes narrowed. "What's the matter, Paris?"

She stalked over to the bedside table, picked up his phone, and threw it at him. When he saw the message, he drew a deep breath.

"Of course I had to make sure you were who you claimed and not some psycho I'm showing around. It was nothing personal."

"Your activities in the shower were quite an interpretation of 'keeping an eye on me.'"

He walked toward her. "Wrong. That was something bigger than both of us. Something that was between us since the first moment we laid eyes on each other."

"Oh?" Paris moistened her lips. How pathetic that she wanted so badly to believe him. He took hold of the lapels of her robe and reeled her in closer. So close she could see the dark flecks in his coffee brown eyes, like slivers of black velvet around the iris. His jaw was smooth and freshly shaved. So that's what he'd been doing in the bathroom. She touched his face lightly with the tip of her forefinger. "You shaved."

He stroked her cheek with the back of his hand. "I'm afraid I may have given you whisker burn earlier. And since I'm not done kissing you . . ."

Action followed word as his mouth moved across hers, teasing and nipping, sending fresh waves of desire rippling through her.

Paris sighed and leaned into him, fighting to keep her head. She needed to find out who had told him to keep an eye on her, and why. And what better way than to play along. After all, two could play this game. He gently sucked her tongue, coaxing it to come play, to explore him the way he explored her, and Paris twined her arms around his neck to pull him closer, inhaling all of him.

Brand tugged her down onto the bed and rolled atop her, his weight held up on his arms while Paris gazed up at him, wondering what he had in mind next.

"I've got an idea," he said, nipping lightly at her earlobe in a way that sent delicious quivers down her neck.

"What's that?"

"Why don't we take a look together at Martha May's journal?"

Paris went from all warm and pliant to frozen stiff in less time than it took him to blink. Damn, he'd rushed things.

"You don't think I'd be dumb enough to bring it with me, do you?"

Fortunately, Brand knew when to pull back. "You didn't bring it?" He made himself sound disappointed.

"Of course not. It's irreplaceable if anything should happen to it."

"I'm sure it is." What was in that damn journal that she didn't want him to see? Maybe Warren was right and she was here hoping to find the deed.

She sat up and tossed her nearly dry hair over her shoulder as if preparing to go. He didn't want her to leave yet and was trying to figure out how to prolong her stay when she spoke.

"I've been dying to see Forked Creek ever since my grandparents died and I came across the journal. What brings you here?"

"Curiosity. Same as you." He stretched out in a relaxed pose.

"Why did you offer to show me around?"

He reached for her slowly; no sudden moves. "Because I think you're cute."

"Right," she said shortly, pulling further back. "No ulterior motives."

He adopted his most innocent tone. "What's that supposed to mean?"

"It means, I might be a librarian, but I can read more than books. You are transparent as glass."

No point hanging on to his aces when the time to play

them was now. "I believe in coming clean. And I know you're not coming clean with me."

"What do you mean?"

"I snooped through your bag at Val's," he admitted. "I know you have the journal." When she turned as if to bolt, he stopped her, turning her back toward him. "I didn't have to tell you that, did I? I just want things to be straight up between us." He watched her closely.

"Just because I brought the journal doesn't mean I'd show it to you."

"You're right on that score. So how about we leave it up to chance? Or Lady Luck."

Paris smelled a setup. How stupid did he think she was?

"What did you have in mind?"

"Ever play billiards?" She wasn't fooled by that innocent little-boy look. What he didn't know was that she had spent many an hour with a billiard cue in her hand, and she never lost.

"Once or twice," she said casually.

"Me too. Mind you it's snooker here. Probably different from what you're used to."

How different could it be? A felt table, some colored balls. "I don't mind giving it a try."

"Great." He rose and flung open the armoire. "You'll have to dress in men's clothing."

"Why?"

"In Forked Creek women have a curfew."

"A curfew?" She laughed. "That's ridiculous!"

"I didn't make the rules a hundred and fifty years ago.

But I can bet the men liked having the freedom to move around while they knew exactly where the women were. Here." Brand dug through the armoire and pulled out a pair of gent's trousers in nubbly beige wool, along with a crisp white shirt and a dark wool jacket. "These look the smallest. Give them a try."

He was disappointed when she pointedly toted the overnight bag into the bathroom with her. No more snooping. He dressed and glanced impatiently at his pocket watch, hoping she wasn't one of those women who took forever to get ready.

The bathroom door opened just a few minutes later, and he wondered why the menswear enhanced her femininity rather than disguised it. He plopped a battered felt hat on her head. "Stick you hair up under this and no one will even guess you're a female."

"Gee, thanks." The gaslight caressed the tawny strands of her hair across her shoulders before she bundled it up under the hat.

"Don't want people to know you're breaking curfew now, do we?"

"Absolutely not. Why else do you think I didn't wear my own jeans?"

Outside, the rain had let up, although the wind whistled around the corners of buildings. It gave the town an eerie feel, compounded by the hollow thud of their footsteps on the wooden sidewalks. The street, for the most part, was deserted.

"It's closed," Paris said in disappointment when they arrived in front of the pool hall.

"Since when do you let the little things stand in your way?"

"Little things like rules and social decorum? I guess always."

"Well, tonight, Paris Sommer, you and I make our own rules."

Picking the lock was child's play, one of his many talents from the Secret Service.

"Isn't that breaking and entering?"

"I look on it more as borrowing something we happen to need."

He pulled the blinds shut across the lone window and switched on the gaslight that hung low over the felt-covered table. Faint accusation deepened the green of her eyes.

"This is a much larger table than for billiards."

"Don't tell me you're going to back down now."

He watched her shoulders straighten beneath the ill-fitting man's jacket. The movement emphasized the snug pull of the white cotton across her generous breasts, reminding him of the sexy, lacy lingerie he'd seen in her bag. "Of course not."

Just thinking about her undergarments gave him an even better idea. "What do you say we up the stakes, make it even more interesting?"

"You want to throw some money on the table, Mister Big Talker? 'Cause I'm in."

"Making it strip snooker would liven things up. Unless, you don't think you can take me."

Her eyes widened in surprise at his suggestion, and he watched her consider her options.

"Sure. Why not?" she said. "It won't be me who's hanging out in my skivvies."

"Heads up!" He tossed her the cue, which she caught expertly in her right hand. He clasped his hand above hers. She did likewise. On it went till they reached the top, where she secured the last hold.

"I break." Her voice rang with triumph.

"Do you want to review the rules?"

"What for? You planning to cheat?"

"I never cheat."

"Good. Then get out of my way."

Her first ball slid into the pocket smooth as silk.

"Nice shot."

"Thanks. And now you lose a piece of clothing." She leaned forward and tipped off his hat with the narrow end of her cue. Her second shot was equally well executed, and she set down her cue to approach him cockily. She unbuttoned his vest and slid it suggestively over his shoulders and down his arms before she tossed it onto a nearby chair. When she picked up her cue and sashayed back to the table, he noted a new, most provocative little wiggle in her walk.

Her shapeless pants took on a life of their own as she leaned across the table. Thong underwear; he'd swear on it. He smiled to himself, confident it wouldn't be long till he found out for sure.

She made her next shot and sank another ball. This time she reached for his shirt buttons, and his eyes never left hers as she nimbly completed the task so she could dip her finger inside and brush his bare skin. He could feel her body heat, smell her excitement, and knew she was getting off on the sense of power.

Her pink tongue moistened her lips suggestively as she tugged his shirttail free of his pants, then slowly slid her hands up over his pectorals. His nipples hardened in response. So did hers. He could see them through the flimsy white shirt. Her pupils dilated and he could hear her breath catch before it speeded up. She tried to draw a deeper breath, but only managed shallow pants, which he knew would throw off her game.

She took her time as her hands moved up to clasp his shoulders and push his shirt free. He was getting aroused just watching her; he loved a confident woman.

"Ready to concede?" she asked.

"Nope."

"Your funeral." She tugged off his shirt and sent it fluttering to join his vest. Then she retrieved her cue and spun in a tight circle, ready to concentrate on her next shot. She faced him and bent across the table, her pose revealing the shadowy swell between her breasts. "One foot on the ground, right?"

"At all times," he agreed, admiring her grace as she sank her next shot.

She faced him triumphantly. "Pants next? Or boots?"

"You'll never get my pants off over my boots, but you're welcome to try."

"Saving the best for last then, are we?"

"Could be. Seeing as how I don't wear underwear."

She cleared three more shots till his boots and socks had joined the pile of his clothing.

"Should we try for a drum roll?" Brand faced her wearing only his jeans and a smile.

"Not necessary." With practiced flair, she sent the ball rolling across the table into the opposite pocket.

"Looks like you got me," Brand said.

She gave him a triumphant smile. "Feel free to leave your pants on, Brand. I made my point."

"That's mighty generous of you," he said. "Seeing how it's my turn to shoot."

"Excuse me? I won fair and square."

"Check the snooker rule book, Princess. I get my turn at the table."

Chapter Four

Paris gnawed her lower lip as Brand leaned over the table and racked the red balls, then positioned the other colored ones along the line at the opposite end of the table. The stained-glass lamp over the table threw his features partly into shadow, emphasizing his blatant, untamed masculinity, and Paris felt a fresh, shocking outpour of desire. How could she possibly feel that way again, so soon?

Cue in hand, Brand adjusted his position. Muscles bunched in his arms and shoulders while the pose did the most delicious thing to the rear of his jeans. If she had so decreed, he would be buck naked right now. She could sidle up behind him and cup those tempting globes in her palms, molding their sleekness, pulling him back hard against her. . . .

She sighed and transferred her attention to the game. A smooth, skillful stroke sent the cue ball down the table to scatter the red balls in a clean break. Just as he'd entered her in one smooth stroke, scattering her inhibitions. Paris had a sneaking suspicion she had met her match, inside and outside the billiard hall.

Her suspicions were confirmed when his first shot sank two balls. She reached up to remove her hat.

"Uh-uh. Boots first."

"Whatever you say." As she sat and bent to untie her boots, Brand knelt before her. He pushed her hands aside and unlaced her sturdy hiking boots.

"I have the feeling this is about to get a lot more interesting." He tugged off her boots, then caressed each delicate foot with his strong hands. The heat of his touch spread up her legs to ignite that feminine part of her above.

He pushed himself to his feet and turned back to the table, and Paris jumped up to watch. This time he sank three balls with a single stroke, something she wouldn't have believed possible if she hadn't seen it with her own eyes. He looked over at her and smirked.

Paris refused to back down. She'd enjoyed lording her brief triumph over him; she'd just have to brazen it out and hope he overplayed his hand.

His eyes skimmed her assessingly. "Shirt first. Nice and slow. Make it last."

Paris had never before removed her clothing while a man watched. Especially when the man watched her with that burning hunger in his eyes—the same hunger that burned through her.

She raised her chin and started on the buttons. Her fingers fumbled and it took a moment to get used to them being on the wrong side.

Next she unbuttoned the cuffs, which she'd folded back because the sleeves were too long. Then she tugged the shirttails free, flicking them playfully in Brand's direction.

She spun around and presented her back to him, legs planted apart as she shrugged her shoulders one at a time and felt the shirt begin a slow slide, inch by torturous inch.

He moved in behind her, his arms around her midsection. His chin brushed her shoulder, his breath warm in her ear. "Very nice." His husky words feathered a shiver down her side to lodge deep in her belly.

His hands looked huge against her ribs, square and sun browned, fingers ridged with calluses from riding or physical labor.

Those same callused palms cupped her breasts through the skimpy lace of her demi-bra. She closed her eyes and leaned back into him. Her nipples ached for his touch; a touch he seemed to deliberately withhold. She could feel his erection harden against her bottom and regretted not stripping him of his jeans when she'd had the chance.

She reached around behind her to cup his balls through the denim, then ran an insistent hand the length of his cock, feeling his instant reaction.

He responded by rolling his thumbs across her nipples. She bit back a moan at the sweet flood of sensation.

He tucked a hand down the front of her pants and she widened her stance to grant him access, allow him to touch that part of her that begged for his attention.

Just when she thought he might actually give her some much-needed release he pulled his hand free, and she bit down hard on her lip in frustration.

He spun her around. "Take your pants off, Paris."

Her eyes never left his as she undid the fastenings. The trousers fell straight to the ground, where she kicked them toward him. He caught them with one hand.

"Nice. Very nice." He tossed them aside and touched the front of her lace thong, then tucked his fingers inside the cup of her lacy bra. Her lingerie was ecru, almost skin tone, and from a distance it would be difficult to ascertain if she wore anything at all.

He cupped her breasts so that they overflowed his touch and then palmed them, arousing the nipples to new pin-points of pleasure and delight.

"Does that make you wet?"

She nodded.

"Say it," Brand ordered.

"That makes me wet," Paris purred.

"I have one more garment to remove, correct?"

She nodded again.

"My choice, right?"

"Your choice."

She was shocked and delighted when he unfastened his

jeans and stepped out of them. His cock jutted toward her, hot and hard and primed for action.

"Turn around and bend over," he said.

She did as she was told, legs apart, elbows braced on the edge of the table. He caressed the warm cheeks of her behind, tugged on the thong string separating them, then moved it aside to reach between her legs. She moved shamelessly against him, sighing with pleasure.

He slid a finger inside her and she moved back and forth, side to side, seeking release.

"Patience, my lovely."

He nibbled the sweet spot between her shoulder and neck and she melted against the table, barely able to support her own weight. His soft velvet tip sought her wetness and teased her.

"This is too good to be rushed." He pushed her hair away to expose her sensitive nape to the torturous teasing of his tongue. He licked and nibbled his way down to her tailbone, his tongue tracing the long, sleek indentation of her spine. Then he knelt to lick the curves of her buttocks, sucking and nipping and fondling her, driving her mad.

She tried to clamp her legs together to lessen the throbbing need, but nothing seemed to help. Brand slid his hands between her thighs and fondled the sensitive crease that separated leg from torso, as he rubbed his cheeks back and forth across the smooth softness of her backside.

"Don't move." He left her briefly, and when he returned he'd sheathed himself in a condom. This time he stroked her soft cleft in teasing circular motions that avoided her throbbing nubbin. She moaned softly as his fingers crept closer and closer, then finally stroked her inside and out, just enough to grant her one quick, shuddering orgasm before he entered her.

"Oh!" It was a moan born of ecstasy and rapture as his slick, hard cock embedded itself deep inside of her. Hands clenched into fists, she braced herself against the snooker table and arched her back, encouraging him to go even deeper, maximizing the friction as he thrust, then withdrew, then thrust again.

As his cock slid smoothly in and out it grazed her clit, triggering an orgasm that burst upon her with wave after wave of shattering intensity, leaving her breathless. She tightened her inner muscles and clenched them around him, both of them throbbing and pulsing in mutual ecstasy.

A scant second later as his hands grasped her hips and turned her slightly, she felt again the determined pressure of his cock filling her, stimulating her anew.

She reached around behind her and gently cupped his balls, rewarded by his sharp intake of breath. His fingers worked magic on the sensitive nerves of her buttocks as he lightly raked his nails up and down while he continued his slow, rhythmic penetration.

She matched his pace, squeezing him tight within as she felt the slow breathless building of another orgasm. He felt it, too, and increased his fervor and changed the angle of his penetration. She felt his balls swell in her palm, and rubbed them ever so lightly. She heard the short shallow breaths that signaled he was getting close to his release, and she raised up on tiptoe to increase the angle of friction.

He released her hips and leaned forward to help himself to her breasts. He circled her sensitized nipples, chafed them against the lace, then finally freed them from the top of the cups.

She heard herself moan, felt the pressure build to unbearable intensity before she released his balls to hone in on her own slippery nub. She exploded and screamed just as she felt him give a final, triumphant surge.

She felt his breath against the back of her neck gradually slow in tandem with hers. His weight across her felt solid and comfortable. He rested his cheek against her spine and kissed her back. Too sated to move, she could barely prop herself against the table.

Just then there was a rattling of the exterior door.

"Ssshhhh . . ." Brand's hand across her mouth muffled her surprised squeal. The blood continued to thunder in her ears as she heard the knob rattle.

"I locked it from the inside; they can't get in."

"Who is it?"

"Probably the sheriff, making sure the town is locked up secure."

They stayed frozen, locked together until Brand released her and reached for his clothes.

"Better get dressed in case they come back."

Paris dove for her pants and shirt and clothed herself in record time.

"There's a back door into the alley. We'll go out that way."

They had just started out the back door when Paris stopped. "My bag," she said. "I left it inside."

She froze at the sound of footsteps and voices at the end of the alley. "I'll distract them," Brand said. "You grab it and go out the front."

Inside the shadowy room, Paris grabbed her bag, slid the lock and stuck her head out the front door. The street was silent and deserted as she slipped from the billiard hall into the welcome shadows of the other buildings. Head down, she walked steadily yet purposefully so she wouldn't call attention to herself.

She wasn't worried about Brand; she was certain he was more than capable of talking his way out of just about anything.

She reached Val's without seeing a soul, and was relieved to find the front door unlocked. She closed it behind her and leaned against its solid weight, glad to make it back undetected.

"You're out late." She jumped as Val emerged from a nearby doorway. "I wondered if you had come in earlier and I'd missed seeing you. Did you know there's a curfew?"

Paris nodded. "I got caught in the rainstorm." She indicated her clothing. "Hence the borrowed clothes."

"You look agitated," Val said. "You must come in and have a brandy."

It was issued more as a command than an invitation, and Paris decided to follow the blonde into the small but tasteful sitting room. A rolltop desk occupied a spot near the window, wing chairs were positioned at a cozy angle to the fireplace, and a sideboard held several liquor decanters and an array of glasses. Val selected two balloon snifters and splashed a generous measure into each.

"I feel I've hardly seen you since your arrival. Is there anything I can do to make your stay more comfortable?"

Paris took a tiny sip of the brandy and felt its burning warmth seep through her. "Nothing I can think of right now, thank you."

"How did you find yourself part of that group you came in with?"

"What gave me away?" Paris asked, hiding her surprise at the other woman's astuteness.

"I've been in the hospitality industry most of my life. I see things others might miss."

"I was a last-minute fill-in," Paris said. "It suits me just fine to be off doing my own thing."

"It's best if you don't explore outside the town, at least not without proper supervision. There are lots of hidden dangers."

Surely nothing more dangerous than Brand and the way he was dominating her thoughts.

Paris shrugged. "I read the waiver before I signed it. I'll be careful."

There was a discreet knock on the door, and a man stepped inside. "I need to talk to you, Val. It's about—"

"Warren," Val cooed sweetly. The way she interrupted him in midsentence made Paris wonder what he'd been about to say. He obviously hadn't noticed her, deep in the wing chair. "Won't you come in and meet one of my ladies?"

"Sorry to interrupt," he said, his eyes lighting on Paris. "I thought you were alone."

"We're just having a nightcap. Won't you join Miss Sommer and me? Paris, this is Warren West, Forked Creek's mayor."

The newcomer looked taken aback, then took a second, more scrutinizing look at her.

Paris rose and extended her hand. "Mr. West. I'm glad we have a chance to meet. Your office implied you were unavailable indefinitely."

He made a smooth recovery as he took her hand and clasped it between both of his in a gesture of welcome. "Things manage to change on an hourly basis in my average day. I'm glad I could get over here."

He slanted Val a look meant to include her. "It seems Miss Sommer has reason to believe she is descended from one of the town's original inhabitants."

"Really," Val murmured. "How interesting. Anyone I might have heard of?"

"Oh yes, indeed. Miss Sommer claims a kinship with Martha May Brown herself."

Paris slid a sidelong glance in the direction of her bag, reassuring herself the journal was safe. For now. But something in the way Warren interpreted her glance, then stared at her directly, sent a frisson of unease up her spine.

"Indeed," Val said. "So Martha May would be your—"

"My great-great-grandmother."

"I wasn't aware she'd had children, were you, Warren?"

"She did leave Forked Creek in the dark of the night, never to be heard from again."

"True. She wouldn't be the first in her profession to start over and claim legitimacy." She addressed Paris. "How fun for you to actually be here in the house where she worked."

"As well as the town where she lived," Paris said. "I'm really looking forward to seeing all of it. I understand your family was instrumental in the restoration, Mr. West."

"It's been a labor of love for the entire clan, starting with old Otis himself."

Otis. The one whose grave had been targeted. She wondered if Warren knew about the incident, then decided it wasn't her place to tell him.

She rose. "Thank you for the brandy, Val. A pleasure to meet you, Mr. West."

He rose as well. "Do call me Warren. And anything you want to know about the town, just ask our Val. She has a wealth of knowledge."

Was it her imagination or did the two of them exchange a pointed look?

"Thank you. I'll try not to be too much of a bother."

"On the contrary, I'm happy to help," Val said.

After leaving Val, Paris passed the main parlor. The sounds of music and laughter from inside receded into the background as she climbed the stairs to her room. Once inside, with the door locked, she sought a safe hiding place for the journal. Beneath her mattress didn't seem secure; neither did the armoire.

As she crossed the room a board squeaked beneath her foot and she dropped to her hands and knees to push back the corner of the carpet. The floorboard was loose. She nearly destroyed her metal nail file prying up the board, but managed to raise it enough to see there was a perfect little cranny beneath. She secreted the journal, then washed her face, stripped out of her borrowed clothing and slipped beneath the sheets, too tired to even look for a nightgown.

Exhausted as she was, sleep remained elusive. Snippets from the day's adventures swam through her head. Meeting Brand. Their erotic shower. The strip-snooker game. In one day, Forked Creek had brought more new adventures than her entire life before.

She felt amazingly free here. No one knew her, and no one had any preconceived notions as to how she ought to act. For once in her life she could seize the moment and follow her instincts.

Paris rolled over onto her stomach, kicked off her covers and cradled her pillow. With her body sexually sated, her mind eventually slowed down, pleasantly numbed by hazy memories of Brand. Memories that would sustain her long after she'd returned to her safe, dull life in Seattle.

Chapter Five

Paris floated in a pleasant dreamlike state, barely conscious of a touch so feather light it could have been real or imagined. The lightest whisper of movement against the soles of her feet was followed by a subtle caress between each toe. It could have been the breeze, or wishful imaginings, but the sensation moved to the ball of each foot. She stirred, absorbing the sensations, having spent far too many years in a life devoid of touch, raised by loving but physically unaffectionate grandparents.

With a sigh, she gave herself over to her feelings and drifted along on a raft of dream longings—longings where the whisper of a breeze turned into a lover's caress. And men like Mitchell Brand rode into her life.

The gliding sensation across her feet turned to dewlike raindrops across the backs of her ankles and calves, a light patter of cool fingertips on overheated skin. Paris sighed, reluctant to waken from the dream.

The divine sensation continued across her thighs to tickle her buttocks before it traced the length of her spine, a spreading warmth that further relaxed her muscles, causing her to sink luxuriously deeper into the feather bed. She felt weightless, boneless, as if the ability to think or to move had leached from her bones and muscles, and all she could do was simply be.

The touch deepened, feeling completely right as pressure points were sought and soothed.

The faint pressure whispered across her shoulder and tickled her spine, before it licked its way back down, over her buttocks and thighs. If this was a dream, it was one she didn't want to awaken from.

Cool hands continued to glide across her skin, skillfully building a new sensation that had become very familiar lately. A slow burn in her belly spread pleasurable warmth throughout her limbs. Her breasts tingled. Nerve endings quivered. Heat and desire banked low in her pelvis and radiated outward, thanks to the talented touch of her phantom.

She continued to drift, giving herself over to the inevitable culmination of deep, consuming sensory pleasure. A tickle between the cheeks of her buttocks made its way to her female lips, teasing them with the promise of more.

Her breathing deepened as the culmination approached, and waves of the most intense pleasure flooded through her and carried her into the beyond.

A short time later, she felt the bed sag with the weight of someone joining her. Instantly awake, she bolted upright and turned to see Brand, who was propped up against a pillow at the headboard. "How did you get in here?"

"I climbed the tree and came in through the window."

"Why?"

"We never got a chance to cuddle afterward in the billiard hall."

Paris leaned over, pulled the sheet up across her bare breasts and tucked it under her armpits, realizing as she did so how ineffectual it was. "You don't strike me as the cuddling type."

He lolled back, his hands behind his head. "You don't know me well enough to reach such a conclusion."

"I know you well enough to know you've been told to keep me in your sights, and will go to any length to do so."

His gaze skimmed her curves beneath the sheet. "And I must say, I'm most certainly liking the sights."

"I was having the most lovely dream before you woke me up."

He rolled close to meet her gaze straight on. "Princess, that was no dream."

Paris frowned. "What do you mean? Of course it was a dream."

He shook his head, reached forward, and barely touched her exposed shoulder.

Paris stiffened. It was a type of touch she'd never forget. The phantom's touch. "How did you do that?"

"Trade secret." Lazily he unrolled himself from the bed and onto his feet. He leaned over and planted a swift kiss on her forehead. "Sweet dreams, Princess. See you in the morning." Then he left her room as soundlessly as he'd entered.

THE SUN HAD BARELY GILDED the tips of the mountains, turning their eggplant tones rusty gold as Paris reached the front doors of the church.

She entered and automatically dipped her fingertips into the basin of holy water, then made the sign of the cross from childhood habit. The church was dark and narrow and smelled of the churches of her youth, aged wood underscored by the faint lingering scent of incense. Sunshine filtered through the narrow stained-glass window and threw shafts of colored light against the nut brown walls.

She walked in the early-morning silence down the center aisle toward the altar, trailing her fingers across the curved wooden pew backs. A huge pipe organ held place of honor at one side of the altar. If she closed her eyes, she could envision scenes from years past: a shyly blushing couple exchanging vows; a fidgety baby being baptized at the stone font; black-garbed, teary-eyed mourners standing near a plain wooden coffin.

Paris paused near a statue of a sad-looking Mary. How different would her own life be if her parents hadn't left her with her grandparents to raise? Would she be less cautious? More free-spirited?

Her grandparents had been strict with her and Paris knew it was because her own parents had been so wild. Part of the "flower child" generation who flocked to San Francisco in the late sixties, they hadn't wanted a baby to interfere with their lives. The few times she'd seen them, they were total strangers to her and she was glad they hadn't kept her. Still, there had always been that hole. . . .That wonder. Why didn't they love her enough to keep her with them? Would anyone ever love her enough to want to share her life, to forge a new life together?

She selected a narrow taper, touched it to a candle flame, and lit a candle in Martha May's memory. Funny that she would feel closer to Martha May here in the church than in the bordello where Martha May had lived and worked. She slid into the second pew and pulled the padded kneeler down, bowed her head and asked for Martha May's help and guidance in deciphering the map and locating the hidden treasure.

Her request completed, she studied her surroundings from a different perspective, surprised at how lonely she felt. She never felt lonely, no matter how much time she spent alone, and she was attempting to identify its cause when Brand suddenly slid into the pew alongside her.

"Sleep well?" he asked innocently.

"Extremely soundly, thank you. How did you know where to find me?"

Brand shrugged. "Not too many places you could go this early."

"Starbucks was my first choice," she said.

Brand grinned. "No 'espresso to go' here."

Why did he have to be so darn appealing, his jaw shadowed with whisker stubble, his eyes bright and clear? "I was actually planning to head to the mine. How far away is it?"

"Which mine?"

She gave him a hard look. "Is there more than one?"

"Well, there's the old silver mine. It's been partly refurbished so some of the corporate groups that come into town can use it for team building and scavenger hunts and the like."

"That doesn't sound like what I'm looking for."

"What exactly are you looking for?"

Paris shrugged. "Just a few different places I read about in Martha May's journal. A revisit of the past."

"Have you seen the photos up at Stewart's yet?"

"No. Who's Stewart?"

"Come on, I'll show you."

Outside, the streets were starting to come to life, a fascinating mix of modern day and yesteryear. The smell of fresh-baked bread and cinnamon wafted over from the General Store, reminding her she was hungry.

Brand could easily walk these streets in any century, Paris thought, with his self-assured stride and air of total control. Was he always so sure of himself? Or was it partly a facade, like her, playing dress-up and finding someone else's clothing more comfortable than her own?

"J. R. Stewart, Photography." She read aloud the sign in the window of the shop Brand stopped in front of.

"Come on." A bell tinkled as they entered the old-fashioned photo parlor and a middle-aged man appeared from behind a black velvet curtain. "May I help you folks this morning?"

"Okay if we look around at some of your work?" Brand asked easily.

"By all means. I'll be in the back if you have any questions."

The walls of the studio were decorated with framed black-and-white photos, and it was impossible for Paris to tell which ones were recent and which ones were more than a hundred years old.

"Over here," Brand said.

The photo showed the bordello, virtually unchanged in appearance, with a group of young women sitting on the steps. "That must be her." With an eerie shiver of recognition, Paris pointed to the woman standing at the top of the steps.

"You look a bit like her."

Paris gave him a look. "The photo's too blurred to tell that."

"I'm betting she had your stubborn streak."

"I'm not stubborn. I'm extremely accommodating with people I like."

He stopped her in front of a wood-framed mirror on the wall and stood behind her, hands on her shoulders. "That woman in the mirror. Do you like her?"

Paris shrugged off his hands and ducked away from the mirror. "What a strange thing to say."

"Not really. I wonder just how well you know yourself. How honest you are with yourself."

"I know myself just fine." The words sounded hollow in her ears. By trying all her life to please others, had she succeeded in pleasing no one, least of all herself?

She stepped forward to study another portrait of the bordello residents. "I wonder why there are so many photos of her and the girls."

"I imagine they were the ones who could afford to have the photos taken. Either that or old J.R. was a steady customer and this is how he paid his tab."

"Look!" She spotted a photo of Martha May in the same room where Paris had, just last night, shared brandy with Val. The furnishings were nearly identical. Martha May was seated at a desk, writing in a book. "Oh my word! It's the journal."

Brand glanced over her shoulder. "The same one?"

"It looks the same." She studied her ancestor closely. "She looks different in this picture. More serene and at peace."

"You've read the journal. What was happening in her life?"

Paris thought for a moment. "Changes. Lots of changes in the works."

"Good changes, if her expression is anything to go by."

If change was good, why had Paris always been so resistant to it?

They were interrupted by the return of the photographer. "Can I interest you in a sitting? A handsome couple such as you ought to have a memento of your visit to Forked Creek."

Brand glanced at Paris. "Thanks. But somehow I feel this is one visit neither of us will ever forget."

He had a point there, Paris thought. She'd arrived at Forked Creek with no idea of what to expect, just knowing she needed to step outside her comfort zone and using the journal as her excuse. Even if there was no pot of gold at rainbow's end, it was fun chasing the rainbow, an adventure to follow the yellow brick road to Oz.

They stepped out into the sunshine. It was decidedly Oz-like here. Brand could be the wizard, working his magic on her. Shaggy Luke could be the cowardly lion, because she sensed something not right about him. Warren West was certainly stiff enough to be the Tin Man. Valerie, she suspected, could play either the good witch or the bad witch, depending on her mood.

The sound of gunshots pulled her from her musings, and she looked up to see they were in front of an old-time open-air shooting gallery. "Is that really a shooting gallery?"

"Every ghost town has one. Ever handle a gun before?"

"Of course not."

He urged her toward the counter. "Then here's your big chance."

"I don't think so. Guns don't interest me."

"Guns were a fact of life here not all that long ago."

"So was poor hygiene. That doesn't mean I have to live that way."

Brand laughed and nudged her closer. "You can't claim to have had the full Forked Creek experience if you don't fire a few rounds."

She eyed him head to toe. "I suppose you also consider yourself part of the full Forked Creek experience?"

"Princess, I am the best part of the Forked Creek experience. Go ahead. Pick it up. See how it feels."

Paris was conscious of the glances coming her way from a few curious onlookers as she stepped up to the wooden counter that stood between her and rows of moving targets. Change wasn't scary, she reminded herself. New experiences were good.

The rifle was heavier than it looked. Her hand felt unsteady as she strove to balance the gun's weight. Brand stepped behind her and his large hands drew her hard against him. As he wedged one leg between hers to widen her stance, Paris burned from the intimacy of his touch. His voice feathered her neck and ear; the heat of his body seared hers. "Balance your weight through the soles of your feet. Feel it?"

All she could feel was him, the way his arms circled her from behind, and her heart pounded crazily at his nearness. She could feel the contraction of his thigh muscles against the backs of her legs as he squatted slightly while his hands guided hers to help raise the gun into position.

"The sight is crooked. You compensate for it by aiming slightly high and to your right."

"Got it."

"Just relax," Brand murmured. His arms brushed the rounded undersides of her breasts and she could feel her nipples harden in response. She caught her breath, aware of a definite male stirring where his body pressed against hers and the way his breathing grew more ragged.

"Now squeeze the trigger ever so gently," Brand said.

As gently as her fingers had stroked and squeezed him. Her hands grew damp at the thought. Her mouth went dry. Her finger found the sleek coldness of the trigger.

She felt the recoil all the way up her arm as the target fell. The immediate rush of power overrode the slow simmer of sexual tension. Right now she was a woman in control, and loving it.

"Good girl. Take your time."

Paris closed her eyes and imagined the two of them taking their time, making love as if they were the only two people in the world, and nothing mattered but their being together.

She opened her eyes and took aim, then squeezed the trigger again. When she missed, a murmur ran through the onlookers.

"Easy," Brand whispered.

It would be easy. Slow and easy, gradually building in intensity, until . . . She fired again and the target fell. This time she was ready for the recoil. It jerked through her with a pleasurable intensity and she resumed her stance. Her finger stroked the trigger with new confidence. She squeezed. Again. And again. Faster. Surer. Until she felt Brand's release and realized she was out of ammunition.

"Well done," he said approvingly.

Paris laid the rifle back on the counter. "I had no idea handling a gun could be so empowering."

"Same as following your instincts. Doing what feels right."

Instinct had brought her to Forked Creek and led her to

Brand. Were instincts something to be trusted no matter what? Or did impulse overshadow instinct?

"Am I an impulse or an instinct to you?" she blurted out.

"A bit of both. And if there's one thing I've learned, there are always consequences to our actions."

The shift was so subtle, if she'd blinked she would have missed it. Without moving an inch, one moment he was by her side, the next he was far away, even as he put his hand on her shoulder.

"I just remembered something I need to take care of," he said.

She stood and watched him walk away, headed toward the livery. He hadn't said a word about seeing her later. Impossible man to attempt to figure out. She really should give up even trying.

INSIDE THE LIVERY, Brand saddled Quicksilver. He was just about to mount up when Warren arrived.

"Where the hell do you think you're going?"

"What does it look like? I'm leaving."

"You can't leave yet. You're not done."

"I am more than done here."

Warren altered his tone. "Brand, I need you."

"You and Elspeth don't need anyone other than your-selves—a fact that was made abundantly clear to me twenty-five years ago."

"I tried to make amends. Why else would I have helped you out a few years ago?"

"Maybe so you'd have a marker to call in? Anyway, I did what you said. I kept her out of the way this morning."

"And you did a great job. The only problem is, the journal wasn't in her room."

"She told me she didn't bring it with her."

"Do you believe her?"

"Maybe." Brand kept his face impassive. "Why would she lie?"

"All women lie."

"True enough. We both learned that one from the best."

A woman's voice said, "Let him leave, the coward. I told you we don't need him." Brand stiffened and turned toward the voice from his past. He ought to have known she'd show up sooner or later.

"Mother, this doesn't concern you," Warren said.

"Everything concerns me." The white-haired woman stepped into the light. She moved more slowly than Brand recalled, but was still a commanding figure. She had to be well into her seventies, yet she appeared nearer to fifty. She must have a hell of a good plastic surgeon, he thought cynically as she faced him straight and tall, her ice blue eyes still full of the bitter hatred Brand remembered.

"You were always a bad seed. Too much of your mother in you."

Brand shrugged. "Personally, I never knew the woman."

"Those of us who knew her wished we hadn't had the pleasure. Including your father. You know why he didn't marry her, don't you? He didn't believe you were his."

Brand refused to rise to her bait. "Whatever you say, Elsie."

"I told you never to call me that."

"I never was much for listening." Brand mounted his horse and turned to face the two of them. "It's been fun, re-visiting old memories."

"What about the deed?" Warren asked.

"If Luke and his cohorts want the town, I say let them have it."

Warren pressed his lips together in displeasure. "I expected better of you, Brand."

"No you didn't. No one ever did."

No one except himself. Quicksilver shifted beneath him, perhaps as impatient as he was to see the back end of Forked Creek. Yet when Brand left town and headed west, the horse hesitated and seemed to urge him east toward the sun-dappled foothills. He'd survived by turning off his feelings, shutting others out, and running when that safety valve no longer worked. Paris was starting to get to him. Only one other person ever had.

"Damn you," Brand swore as he gave his mount his head. If Old Smyth was still out there, trust Quicksilver to know where.

Besides, it had been far too long since he'd been out like this with the sun overhead, the saddle beneath him, and not a care in the world. Well, hardly a care in the world.

Truth be told, he'd never known the meaning of *carefree.* Life with his father had been quiet and sad. After marrying Elsie, his father just seemed to grieve himself to death slowly—something Brand would never forgive him for, along with not doing right by his mother. Elsie had enjoyed calling him a bastard every chance she got, almost as much as she'd enjoyed shipping him off to that military college and washing her hands of him.

He rode farther into the hills, letting Quicksilver pick his way.

"Hey!" When a bullet whizzed past his head, he pulled up short and surveyed the countryside. He didn't have to wait long for a slouchy-looking horse and rider to appear out of nowhere.

"Ya filled out some," Smyth said at length, after they had each silently taken the other's measure, same as they had all those years ago.

"You haven't," Brand said. The old man was as whipcord lean and leathery as ever. "Why'd you take a shot at me?"

"You know it's my way of greeting folks who come out this way uninvited."

"Quicksilver seemed to think we were invited."

"Didn't I teach y'all better than to be blaming the horse?"

"Among other things."

Their horses fell into step together with no particular destination.

"Next you'll be telling me hell froze over."

"Something like that."

"Sure as shooting you aren't back here 'cause of her."

Brand exhaled impatiently. He shouldn't have to justify his presence. "I owed Warren. Plain and simple."

"Don't tell me you're still holding the lad's mother against him."

"Nah. I'm better than that."

"Not Warren's fault your pa loved your ma way better than he loved Elspeth."

Brand felt a flash of emotion he didn't want to feel. "So why the hell did he marry Elsie?"

"Don't tell me you never figured that one out. Elspeth had means, and your old man wanted to make as good a life for you as he could. He thought having a family and a brother would be good for you."

"You're telling me he married that bitch because of me?" Brand barked out a humorless laugh. "Isn't that just one of life's little ironies?"

"How's tricks down there?" Smyth cocked his head in the direction of Forked Creek.

Brand shrugged.

"Even living up here, I hear things. Lamoy and his bunch."

"Why don't you go ask Warren if you're so interested?"

Smyth cocked his head and gave Brand a searching look. "Always could read you like a book, you know."

"It's nothing to me. None of it."

"If you say. I tried to teach you not to high-tail away from stuff just 'cause it makes you uncomfortable." Smyth gave a slow head shake that punctuated the disappointment in his eyes.

In spite of himself, Brand felt defensive. "You know the day I left I swore I'd never be back."

"Should know better than to swear to something like that."

"Yeah, well . . . What the hell?"

For there in the distance, looking as if she were out for a Sunday stroll, was Paris.

"Friend of yours?" Smyth asked.

It was a question Brand had no idea how to answer.

Chapter Six

Still smarting from the way Brand had left her right after the foreplay of the shooting gallery, Paris wasn't pleased at the immediate frisson of excitement that tingled through her. He sat the horse as if he'd been born to the saddle, and looked totally at home in this rugged, untamed landscape.

She ignored him to focus on his companion, a grizzled, leathery man of undetermined age who watched her with a faint grin, his eyes traveling from her to Brand and back to her.

"Are you from around these parts?" she asked sweetly.

"Could say."

"Then you must know where the hot springs are. Am I

getting close?" Her impression from Martha May's journal entry *Hope springs eternal,* was that the hot springs held a clue to her hunt.

He flashed her a wary look. "Tourists don't know about the springs."

Brand spoke up. "Paris is kin to one of the original settlers. She's here on some secret mission based on Martha May's journal."

"Martha May was one smart lady, by all accounts. Perhaps you'd best see her there, Brand."

Paris didn't miss the pointed look Brand sent the old-timer, and piped up quickly, "I wouldn't dream of imposing on Brand's time."

"Any man who doesn't have time for a pretty woman is a sad creature indeed."

Brand shot him an impatient look. "I don't recall seeing any pretty women in your life."

"There's some areas a fellow learns to practice discretion. I'd peg this as one of those times."

"Oh you would, would you?"

Paris felt a flash of impatience. "Would one of you please just direct me to the springs?"

Brand heaved a sigh. "I'll take you."

"That's not necessary," Paris said stiffly.

The older man laughed. "She's a stubborn one, Brand. *Must* be kin to Martha May."

"Did you know Martha May?" She realized as soon as she spoke just how silly that must sound. "I'm sorry. Of course you didn't; you're not nearly that old."

The older man's laugh sounded more like a rusty cackle. "My gran knew her. Gran was friends with everyone."

"I take it Martha May didn't have many friends?"

"That's how it was back then. An independent business woman wasn't exactly embraced by the town wives."

Brand said. "But now Forked Creek is hell-bent on being the last bastion of old-fashioned chivalry. I'll take you to the springs."

"How do you know the way?" she asked.

"Been through here a time or two. A long time past." He dismounted in an easy fluid motion and gestured for her to take his place. When she hesitated, he said, "It's narrow going. It'll be better if I lead Quicksilver."

"I'll walk, too, then."

Brand crossed his arms over his chest. "If you want my help getting there, you do as I say. Now let's go."

Paris pursed her lips, but good sense won out. She wanted to reach the hot springs more than she wanted to fight with Brand, and with his assistance she managed to clamber into the saddle with slightly more grace than last time. He took the reins, shook hands with his friend, and led her and the horse east, into the hills.

Looking back over her shoulder, Paris could just make out the town nestled in the valley. It looked almost too perfect to be real, like an artist's depiction of a nineteenth-century Western mining town.

The way wasn't either narrow or hazardous and as she watched Brand's easy stride ahead of the horse she wondered why he had chosen not to ride. Perhaps he was already regretting their recent intimacy, having fulfilled his orders to "keep an eye on her."

They hadn't traveled very far before the mountain breeze teased her nostrils with the unmistakable odor of sulphur.

"We must be close—I can smell them."

"Just up ahead."

Paris was glad to have her heightened vantage point to take in the sight of the handful of steaming pools, nearly perfectly round, as if they'd been cut into the rocks with a giant cookie cutter. Brand brought the horse to a stop and she swung her leg over the saddle to dismount, only to find Brand there. She slid into his arms as if she had every right to be there, as if it was the only place she wanted to be.

"Is this what you were looking for?" he asked in husky tones.

She didn't step away. She couldn't. Not when she was drowning in the coffee-dark pools of his eyes, more enticing than any hot springs. She could see herself reflected in their thickly lashed depths, and it was as if she was a part of him as much as he was a part of her.

"I think it just might be," she said. Her words were so low he had to dip his head forward to hear them. From there it seemed only natural that his lips would find their way to hers. She exhaled with a soft sigh as he sealed the kiss, branding her.

His lips were warm, shaping hers with a possessive knowledge that sent shivers of delight through her veins. He clasped her against him in a way that silenced any notion he regretted their previous encounters; his body was clearly recalling the pleasure of their joining as much as hers. She felt like wax, softening in the heat of his embrace as his body grew hard against hers. Insistent. Demanding.

She swayed toward him as if guided by inner forces, loving the way the rounder contours of her body fitted themselves to the planes and angles of his. The throbbing, needful juncture of her thighs interlocked with his. The hardness of his arousal, even through their clothing, made her insides weep for more.

He undid the buttons on her cotton blouse and her nipples hardened with impatience to feel the urgent brush of his callused fingertips.

He buried his face in the valley of her cleavage and drank in her scent in a long, greedy gulp that ended on a growl of impatience. He flicked open the front fastening of her bra and pushed her breasts together, intent on devouring them both at once.

Paris gave a half moan, half sigh at the way his hungry mouth ravaged her softness. She threaded her fingers through his hair and hung on, her head back, eyes closed, all her senses fully alive. Everything felt doubly intense—the warmth of the sun, the smell of the sulphurous springs, the birdsong that trilled through the stillness of the countryside.

Finally sated, Brand transferred his attention back to her neglected lips. This kiss was softer, as if the softness of her breasts, the way she gave them so freely, had tempered the hard edge of his impatience. He ran his hands down her back and possessively fondled her bottom before moving up to the curve of her shoulders.

"It's considered bad luck if one visits the springs and doesn't test their curative powers."

Paris linked her fingers behind him, absorbing his strength and support. "You mean total immersion?"

"Mmmmmmmm . . ." He nuzzled her neck. His tongue darted out to find the beat of her pulse. "Total naked immersion. You game?"

Paris hesitated. The idea of the two of them naked in the hot spring held a lot of appeal, but she couldn't lose sight of why she was here. Martha May had written, *"Hope springs eternal."* What sort of clue was that supposed to be?

"I take it that's a yes?" Brand pushed her blouse off her shoulders and she felt the contrast of the sun's rays and the cooler mountain air caressing her skin.

She tugged her blouse back on. "You go ahead. I want to explore a bit."

Brand subjected her to a long, searching look. "Suit yourself. You don't know what you're missing."

Paris shrugged lightly, then turned and went past the main spring-fed pool to a second, smaller one, buttoning her blouse as she went. The rock formation was like nothing she had ever seen before, the color and texture of reddish brown sand, yet hard and smooth to the touch. The area was littered with several hollows, ranging in size from basin to bathtub to party-size hot tub. Hot springs fed only a handful of the holes; the rest were empty, forming an unusual landscape.

Here and there she came across loose rocks that she shifted aside. Did she really expect to find something hidden beneath them? She could look forever around here and still miss whatever she was supposed to find.

She climbed upward with no particular destination in mind. She paused at one point and looked back to where Brand lolled in the largest spring. His arms rested on the edge of the pool, head back, eyes closed. He seemed as much a part of this landscape as if he'd been born to it. He belonged here. She didn't. Paris found herself beginning to doubt she belonged anywhere.

As she began her descent back to Brand, she saw a carving—a cross and triangle that had been carved into the rock. Below the symbols were letters followed by a familiar date, one matching a late entry in the journal. Was it significant or was she grasping at straws?

She returned to the hot pool where Brand relaxed, squatted down, and dipped her fingers in to test the temperature. Moving so quickly it was a blur, he grabbed her hand and laid it flat against his chest. Paris recoiled, teetered on the edge, then toppled forward with a yelp of surprise.

Brand caught her, scooped her into his arms, and held her close. She struggled to get free, splashing him when he had the nerve to laugh at her.

"Naked really is better," he said. "Why wouldn't you believe me?"

Paris gave up her flailing to join his laughter. The water felt wonderful. Suddenly all cares and anxieties evaporated as if they'd never been. She was on a life-changing adventure and right now she was in the arms of the sexiest man she'd ever met. She tugged off her boots and tossed them onto dry land.

"Sometimes I'm a slow study."

"But you know when to stand firm and when to acquiesce."

"This seems one of those times I surrender to your lead."

"Very wise," Brand said. "I have to tell you, though. It's much easier to get out of your clothes when they're dry."

"No one ever accused me of doing things the easy way."

The warmth in his gaze was melting hers. "Most definitely, nothing about you is easy."

This time, when he unbuttoned her blouse and peeled down the sleeves, she enjoyed the sensation of him unwrapping her as if she were a wonderous gift. Brand had a way of making her feel special and beautiful, and she felt as if she'd waited all her life to experience it.

Her blouse discarded along with her bra, he hooked his fingers in her waistband and wrestled her wet jeans off.

"I've never skinny-dipped before," Paris confessed. "I feel so free."

Brand spun her around so she was straddling his lap, and she tangled her fingers through his hair. The damp ends were starting to curl.

"It's basic," Brand said. "Just you and the elements of nature."

Brand was truly one of nature's basic elements. Unchallenged and untamed. Eminently capable. She recalled the first time she laid eyes on him, the way he'd gentled the skittish horse. Was he applying those same gentling techniques to her, gradually winning her trust?

Could she trust him?

He touched the corners of her mouth with his fingertips. "Deep thoughts lead to frown lines."

"You're right," Paris said. "I'd far sooner have laugh lines."

"The other option is love lines."

"Ah," Paris sighed. "Elusive love. Have you ever been in love?"

"Never. You?"

She shook her head. "I thought so once, but now I'm not even sure I believe in it. Passion, yes. But love?"

"Passion's good." His eyes never left hers as he cupped her breasts lightly and allowed her nipples to barely brush his palms.

His light touch sent fire racing through her, as if he'd touched match to tinder. He slowly moved his hands in ever-widening circles and teased her nipples, turning them into a wellspring of pleasure that radiated through her breasts to her belly, where it settled into her feminine recesses with a warm glow.

She arched her back and leaned into him, increasing the pressure, awash in sensation, Brand's bare skin against hers as they shared the soothing water of the springs. Overhead, the sun warmed the delightfully fresh mountain air. Sensations within and without stimulated her to new heights of appreciation for being alive, for being a woman here with Brand.

His shoulders were broad and ridged with muscle. She watched the sinewy pull of those intriguing muscles beneath satiny skin as he cupped a handful of water and trickled it slowly over her shoulder to watch the way rivulets coursed over her skin and found a pathway between her breasts.

He gently kneaded her shoulders and she groaned softly when he found the knot of tension at the base of her skull. "Turn around, I'll give you a back rub."

"Like last night?"

"Princess, that was no back rub. That was a Mitchell Brand special."

He picked her up and spun her around, nesting her between his thighs on the pool's natural rock ledge. She planted her hands on his legs to brace herself as he began to massage the back of her neck.

As his powerful fingers found and pressed key tension points in her neck and shoulders, she raked the skin of his thighs with her nails. As his hands moved to her spine and shoulder blades and began to ease the tension stored there, she flattened her palms and moved them in a light caress, enjoying the way his muscles tensed and his hair-roughened skin teased her sensitive fingertips.

Behind her, his cock slowly lengthened and thickened until it pressed insistently against the spot where her spine curved into her bottom. Her insides tensed and tingled in anticipation. Awash in the magic wrought by his touch, she shifted and felt his instant response. What heady power, to know that he was affected as much as she was.

He wrapped his hands around her middle and pulled her back hard against him. His hands slid from her waist to her breasts and she felt an instant restless yearning between her legs.

His hands slid smoothly down her ribs and stomach, over her Venus mound, and through the curls to gently coax her legs apart.

As his fingers slid across her throbbing pearl to the opening petals of her inner lips, Paris gave a tiny gasping sob.

"Easy." Brand spoke from behind her, raised her up slightly on his lap for easier admittance. His warm breath feathered her ear and sent pinpricks of awareness dancing deep inside.

"We need to get the rest of you relaxed." Brand continued to speak in soothing tones as he eased his fingers deeper into her inner softness.

Paris moved with him, in desperate need of the release so near. She pulsed and throbbed, her inner muscles tightening greedily around him. His thumb grazed her opening while his fingers found the right rhythm of entry and withdrawal.

She was aflame. On fire.

At his urging she first leaned hard against him, then forward away from him, changing the angle at which his fingers entered and stimulated her.

"I want you. All of you." She could feel his cock against her back, hard and hot and as hungry for her as she was for him. Abruptly, impatiently she lifted herself off his hand, turned around, and attempted to mount him.

He held her back, then stood, and lifted her clean out of the pool, setting her on the edge. "Are you always this impatient?"

"When I know what I want." His cock faced her, primed and ready. She reached for him. Her insides ached for the sweet sensation of him pushing inside of her and taking possession of her fully. He avoided her reach, then pushed her legs apart and knelt before her.

Paris leaned back on her elbows and stared upward at the bluest of cloudless skies overhead as Brand started licking the soft inner skin of her thighs, then slowly nibbled his way toward the promised land. Her entire body had become an out-of-control erogenous zone. She bent her knees, arched her back, and ran the sensitive sole of one foot across his back and over his shoulder to his ear. He caught her foot and licked it, his tongue like wildfire across the delicate arch.

"I'm dying here," she said.

"Dying only to be reborn." His hands on her thighs, Brand moved closer. "That's why the French call the orgasm 'petit mort,' 'little death.'"

Paris moaned as he buried his face between her legs, his breath hot, his tongue even hotter as it traced the outline of her pouty outer lips and played hide-and-seek with her sensitive inner lips, before finally, gently, laving the swollen bud of her clitoris.

The first orgasm hit like a tidal wave. Paris bucked beneath him with a shriek as his tongue dipped inside of her and drank in her essence. She barely felt herself throb and clench before the second wave hit, followed by a third, leaving her weak and shaking. Her cries of pleasure were still echoing off the mountains as Brand scooped her back down into the hot pool, secure in his embrace.

Chapter Seven

Paris clung weakly to Brand as her breathing gradually slowed to near normal. Brand wondered if he'd ever breathe normally again. He'd never known a woman to give it up like that—and he'd known plenty of women, lots of whom enjoyed sex as much as he did. None could rival Paris and the way she held back nothing.

Brand wasn't sure if she was to be pitied or envied even as he wondered what it must be like to experience such total lack of control. Unthinkable for him, who'd honed his survival island by not giving away anything he didn't have to.

He liked it that way. What he didn't like was the way Paris was getting him to look at things differently.

He shifted to face the woman in his arms. Right now, what he had was hers, and he was fully primed to ensure Paris got everything he was capable of. Even if it didn't seem like much. What shook him was that he wanted to do more for her, more than he'd ever done for anyone before.

"Feeling better?"

Wordlessly she nodded. Her eyes still had that glazed-over look and he couldn't resist pressing a kiss to each trembling lid. He ran his thumb across her swollen lower lip until her lips parted, just wide enough that he could play. He teased the tip of her tongue and the ridge of her teeth, then slid his thumb in and out of her mouth suggestively as if it was a different part of his body, a part that even now was achingly hard and arced toward her, begging to be buried deep inside her velvety wet warmth.

Patience. He'd have his release, but not now, not quite yet.

Paris was a quick study. Her energy magically renewed, she sucked enthusiastically on his thumb, alternated with sweeping motions of her tongue that drove him mad, only imagining that sweet darting tongue attending to his cock and balls. Next she swung around to straddle him. She brushed the tips of her nipples teasingly across his chest, back and forth and up and down in ever-widening circles. Exquisite torture, as her nails simultaneously lightly raked his back and shoulders. He cupped the globes of her ass and shifted her to a more accessible position on his lap, so near and yet so far from the head of his cock.

She took firm hold of it and slid her fist slowly and lovingly down its length, from aching tip to sensitive nest, where her other hand fondled his balls.

Brand sucked in his breath and concentrated on the sweet torture of her touch. He enjoyed the way her thighs gripped his, her ass so enticingly near, while her breasts peeked shyly up at him from just below the water. He fondled their lush fullness and felt the tight nipples respond and mold to his palms as her lips found his.

It was a sweet kiss, one where she gave and gave, pouring soothing care and warmth over the grown-over scar tissue of his past. Her body enfolded his, fit him like hand to glove, and he shifted, primed for entry, when she moved as well.

Instead of finding himself embedded deep within her, somehow she angled his throbbing cock till it was pressed against her vertically, then began to slide herself up and down his shaft. He could feel the hot greedy kiss of her nether lips, the demanding pulse of her clit, and her hungry opening, all sliding up and down the sensitive underside of his cock.

Using her feet for leverage, she increased the speed at which she moved, riding him up and down at a frenzied pace. He gulped when he heard her soft sob of pleasure, followed by the undulating ripples of the aftershock as she came again. Brand feared he was going to explode, right then and there, without even having been inside of her.

Suddenly she stopped and pressed her lips to his ear. "No you don't. Not yet."

"Princess, a man can only take so much!"

She gave a teasing little jiggle. "Don't you want to be in me?"

He grabbed her ass and squeezed. "What do you think?"

"I want you filling me too. But first I want to taste you."

Brand rose swiftly to his feet, his eager buddy ramrod straight in front of him, praying his legs would support him.

Her breasts bobbed as she bent over to reach him. Delicately, her small pink tongue darted out and swept across the glistening glans of his shaft. He trembled and forced himself to stand perfectly still as she closed her lips over him. He heard her murmur against him as she took him into her mouth, one inch, then a second, followed by a little more, her tongue continuing to make that divine swirling motion against him, before she gently licked his balls. He jerked against her, his concentration centered solely on control.

This was all wrong, the way she had suddenly gained the upper hand. Abruptly he picked her up and turned her around so her backside faced him, the beautiful white moon of her ass urging him on.

Obviously of a similar mind, she braced herself on the lip of the pool and angled her body toward his. It was all the invitation he needed to enter her in one swift stroke. She was so hot and wet and tight, he felt as if he were being swallowed whole. His moan of pleasure echoed hers. It was too damn good and he wanted it to last. He slowed to a stop and concentrated on naming the fifty U.S. states in his mind.

Back in control once more, he deliberately increased his pace, finding the perfect angle of entry. He knew he'd hit her g-spot when he felt her come apart, nearly drowning his cock with a warm gush of female fluid. Faster, he drove himself into her and felt his balls slap the backs of her legs as he caressed her ass and emptied himself into her, awash in her echoing moans of supreme satisfaction.

He clasped her around the waist and sank back down to the stone ledge, carrying her with him. She curled up against him as if she'd been doing it all her life.

He nuzzled her neck, tonguing the rapidly beating pulse. "Darlin' where have you been all my life?"

"Seattle. You?"

He'd been to hell and back, not something he was about to spoil the afterglow with. But for the first time, he was tempted to share his past.

"Here and there. I never stayed anyplace too long."

"Where's the most interesting place you've been to?"

Pillow talk was a game he could play. "I'm thinking right here, right now with you."

"You!" She spun about and sent a rippling splash of water his way.

"What?"

"I know evasion tactics when I hear them." She climbed from the pool.

"Where are you going?"

"I don't know about you, but I'm starting to prune. And my clothes are soaking, thanks to you."

"Can I help it if you're skittish?"

"That mare you tamed the other day was *skittish*. If you spooked her the way you spooked me, you'd have a horseshoe between the eyes."

"Horses are a damn sight easier to read than a woman. Hey! What are you doing?"

"Helping myself to your jeans and your shirt."

"What am I supposed to wear back to town?"

"I would recommend your boxers and chaps. Lucky thing you wore underwear today."

"Lucky for you, you mean. 'Cause if one of us was heading back bare-assed today, it sure wouldn't be me."

He clambered from the pool, unable to keep a little strut from his walk. He felt as cocky as a rooster in the henhouse, with good reason.

On the heels of his thoughts, he felt his Johnson begin to make the quickest recovery in history. Lazily he stretched and welcomed the sun's caress, loving the way it dried his skin. He felt more relaxed, more replete than he could ever recall before.

Across from him, her eyes widening in disbelief as he grew hard all over again, Paris looked unbelievably sexy wearing nothing but his denim shirt.

He started toward her. "I'm not so convinced I feel like loaning out my shirt."

"Too bad! I've got first dibs!" Paris couldn't say what made her turn tail and scamper off. Maybe it was the look in Brand's eye. It certainly wasn't the fact that he was obviously aroused all over again. Could a man really recover so quickly? Obviously Brand could!

She followed a different path than last time, one that wound around behind some caves and brush. The ground here sported fuzzy, half-starved mountain grass. She zigged in an attempt to lose Brand, only to skid to an abrupt halt.

Directly across her path, suspended between a rocky outcropping and a spindly tree, was a canvas hammock.

When she reached out and touched it, the ropes squeaked as it swayed. It seemed solid enough and the rope securing it looked fairly new. In fact, it looked suspiciously like the rope Brand had used that first day as he subdued the horse.

She spun around as he approached. "I don't suppose you know anything about how this got here, do you?"

Brand shrugged carelessly and dropped into the hammock, stacked his arms beneath his head like a makeshift pillow and closed his eyes. Was he always that trusting? Or did he know it was secure because he'd made it so?

"I don't know who's responsible for the hammock, but I don't look a gift horse in the mouth." His tone softened beguilingly. "Come over here."

"I have to get going."

"It's a long walk back to town."

"I like to walk."

"Paris, you don't know the way. You don't even have a bottle of water or a compass."

"I'll find the way. I'm very capable."

"Don't you ever do anything on impulse?"

Paris stared in at him, hands on hips. *Yes—this entire trip.* The interlude in the shower. In the billiard hall. In the hot springs. She had been more impulsive in the past twenty-four hours than in her entire lifetime.

Brand stared pointedly to where his penis lay flaccid against his thigh. "Look. You've gone and scared him away."

Paris could only shake her head. She'd never known anyone like Brand. A man who could walk around unclothed outdoors, totally comfortable in his skin. Comfortable in himself, casually discussing sex as if it were the weather.

"Listen," Brand said.

Obediently Paris concentrated. She didn't hear a thing.

"You need to close your eyes."

"I'm not here to play games, Brand."

"Princess, neither am I."

Her eyes flew to his. Something in his tone triggered all sorts of warnings. Steely determination met her gaze. This was a new side of Brand, a man whose tone, whose entire pose brooked no nonsense. A man who could, if circumstances demanded it, prove dangerous.

"I'd never hurt you."

Paris shuddered. Could he read her mind?

"Not even if you were ordered to? Just as you were told to keep an eye on me?"

"No one tells me what to do. Not anymore."

"Who are you, Mitchell Brand?"

He shook his head. "I don't have the answer to that."

"Who did you used to be?"

"Just a man. A man intent on doing what has to be done."

"Am I something that has to be done?"

"I think maybe you are. Now come on over here."

A magnetic field seemed to draw her slowly, inexorably toward the man; she felt as if something significant was about to happen. The emotional intimacy both fascinated and frightened her, like a moth drawn to a flame.

Brand took her hand and coaxed her into the hammock,

where she stretched out beside him. He gently set them to rocking.

"There now, isn't that nice?" His arms cradled her close and his shoulder pillowed her head. He ran a hand slowly through her hair and lifted a strand to take a deep, appreciative sniff.

"Lilacs?" he asked.

"Lilac shampoo," she said.

"From now on, anytime I smell lilacs I'll be reminded of you."

"I get the feeling that once we're both gone from here, you won't much like being reminded of me."

"But I won't be able to forget you."

And with that, Paris knew she would have to be content.

As she turned to face him, the hammock rocked and she found herself sprawled atop him. His response was instant and very male as he hardened and thickened against her bare thigh. His hands cradled her naked backside beneath the softly worn denim of his shirt, molding the softness of her curves.

In spite of herself, Paris became flooded with fresh desire. Brand's hands continued their journey beneath the shirt, past her waist and up her back, gently coaxing every nerve ending to total awareness of the primal male beneath her. She raised herself up slightly and glanced down at him. His pupils dilated, his breath caught, and she was lost, swept away on a wave of need and desire.

Their mouths met and clung in mutual hunger and need, a dark, needful place where desire overtook all else. She needed him. Needed his lips devouring hers, finding and reshaping their softness as his lungs filled hers with life-giving oxygen. Life-giving Brand. Blood coursed through her veins as she tangled her limbs with his, her pelvis moving with him, against him, exciting them both to heightened prisms of desire.

He shifted her so she straddled him, her knees on either side of his waist. She sat up and ran her hands across his chest, absorbing its planes and contours, the well-developed pectorals, the crisp matting of hair, the way his flat male nipples hardened beneath her fingertips. His eyes darkened with desire as she touched him freely.

He followed her lead, his hands burrowing beneath the shirt to her breasts, where he teased her nipples. Her body responded with a fresh outpouring of heated desire that he couldn't help but be aware of.

She watched him wet his lips with his tongue, his eyes never leaving hers, his mouth open wide in invitation. An invitation she was powerless to resist. She unbuttoned the borrowed shirt, baring her breasts to Brand's gaze and the silent countryside before she leaned forward from the waist and dragged them across his face. His hot breath anointed them seconds before his eager tongue and lips paid them homage. He opened his mouth wide as she swayed from side to side, teasing him and herself, till finally she surrendered, allowing him to pull each turgid nipple into his mouth.

He suckled deeply, sending an answering tug of desire through her. As he sucked her breasts, she swayed against him. Her breath rose and fell in short, sharp gasps; she was streaming wet; her sweet spot pulsed, demanding release.

Frantically she rubbed herself against him, dampening him

with her juices to ensure easier entry before she slowly lowered herself upon him. She gasped with relief as he filled her with the sweetest sensation she had ever known. Abruptly she stopped, her eyes startled as they met his.

He didn't move a muscle.

"Protection," she gasped out. "We didn't use anything earlier, either."

"Do we need it?"

"I'm on the pill."

"Anything else I ought to know about?"

She shook her head. "You?"

"Clean as fresh-fallen snow."

Her tension evaporated, replaced with heightened desire. She could feel him embedded deeply inside her, and tightened her internal muscles. "Thank goodness. I don't know if I could stop."

"So don't. No, do."

"Do . . . what? This?" She gloved him even more tightly. "Or this?" She arched her back, altering the angle of entry, then pivoted forward, her hands on his chest supporting her weight as she settled in for the ride. His shaft slid across her clitoris and she reared up and sucked in her breath.

"Don't fight it," Brand said.

"I'm afraid of setting you off too soon. I want it to last."

"You don't have to worry about that. I'll last as long as you need me to."

How about forever?

Except men like Mitchell Brand didn't spend forever with anyone.

She concentrated on the sensations inside of her—the sweet building of pressure as she swiveled her hips, first side to side, then in slow deliberate circles, careful not to allow too much friction as she kept him firmly embedded. The hammock swayed gently beneath them, increasing the stimulation.

He reached up and palmed her breasts.

"Now this I could do all day." He arched his back, driving himself even more deeply inside.

"Bet you couldn't." Paris responded with a thrust of her own.

"I sure would like to try." Back and forth, up and down— despite her earlier words about wanting it to last, she couldn't seem to help herself. She clung to him, rode him with a frantic, desperate energy to a place where nothing existed save her and Brand. There was no surrounding countryside, no journal and map. Her entire focus centered on the final lap, the beat before the crescendo of orgasmic release.

She reached down to where their bodies were joined and fisted his cock, adding that friction to the rhythm of the ride. He moaned aloud and increased his pace. Her hold on him heightened the pressure to her clitoris as her hand and body slipped up and down his swollen cock. She was wetter and hotter than she'd ever been in her life. Tiny ripples started to lap at her, radiating out through her limbs.

"Not yet. Not yet," she managed to gasp between moans of mounting pleasure, a pleasure so intense, it sucked the breath from her lungs, stole the blood from her veins, and finally ripped through her with intense force, completed by Brand's final thrust and cry of release.

Chapter Eight

Brand seemed no more inclined than she to chatter on the ride back to town, which suited Paris perfectly. She appreciated the time to digest the significance of the carving she'd discovered at the springs. M.M.B. along with the date, MAY 13, 1868, and what appeared to be a cross next to a triangle. The Trinity? The date could be significant as it was a time toward the end of Martha May's journal, shortly before she left Forked Creek for good.

The cross part baffled her. Paris doubted Martha May was a churchgoer, since she wasn't exactly living a clean and wholesome lifestyle. Did the cross refer to the church, the graveyard, or maybe just a plea to the higher powers? And what did the triangle mean? Was Martha May part of a love triangle? Was the symbol her way of asking forgiveness?

Paris snuck a quick look at Brand behind her. His gaze was focused far in the distance and she half-wished she was able to confide in him, to brainstorm her findings aloud, but she had no idea whether or not he could be trusted.

"Where were you headed when I saw you earlier today?" she asked him.

"No place special. Away from here."

"And now?"

"For now, Princess"—he flashed her a sexy smile that made her insides tingle—"you keep giving me one more reason to stick around."

"Don't feel obliged to change your plans on my account."

"Believe me, my plans are my own. And right now they happen to include you."

"Because you were told to."

Brand blew out a long breath that stirred the hair on the back of her neck. "Do you always take things at face value?"

"That usually proves the best way."

"Listen, I'm going to drop you off at the bordello and nose around a bit on my own, see what I can find out that might prove of interest. We can pool our resources later tonight, so wait in your room till I get there. And don't be saying much to Valerie."

"She's going to see you dropping me off," Paris said. For up ahead, basking in the late-afternoon sun on the porch, were half a dozen of Paris's group along with their hostess.

"Just remember what I said. I'll be back later."

"DON'T TELL ME YOU WENT and found yourself a hand-some, rugged cowboy?" Hayley teased, as Paris clambered off the horse and climbed the wide front stairs to join the others.

"Yes, do tell," Valerie said. "He's definitely a new face in these parts."

Paris tried for a nonchalant shrug. "You said it yourself. Forked Creek is a place where anything can happen."

"Well, don't be doing an exclusive," said a dimpled perky blonde whose name Paris didn't remember. "No point in having all your eggs in one basket."

There was a round of good-natured laughter.

"I adore make-believe," said Hayley. "How long has the town been operating like this?"

"It originally opened in the sixties," Val said. "At that time it catered solely to corporations looking for a unique lo-cale to bring their management teams. Everyone loved the place and the atmosphere so much, they wanted to come back with their families. Under the new CEO, Warren West, who is the acting mayor as part of his duties, the town evolved to what you see today."

Warren West, Paris mused. The man she'd met here the other night. The one who hadn't responded to her original request for information on the town's history.

"Mr. West's family, starting with a man called Otis Lam, is one of the original owners of the mine and the town that grew up around it. It's been a labor of love for several generations to bring the town to the standards you are currently enjoying."

"What of the rumors of a modern conference center going up nearby? Won't that destroy the integrity of Forked Creek?"

"Not at all," Valerie said smoothly. "If anything it ought to enhance what's here and offer more amenities for groups who require them."

"I can think of a few amenities I require," cracked one of the girls.

Valerie smiled. "We'll see what we can do to meet all of your needs."

THE FELLOW AT THE LIVERY had taken one startled look at him and skittered away, which ought to have told Brand that something weird was afoot. But the instincts that had kept him alive all those years in the military seemed to have gone to sleep due to sexual satiation.

Which was how he came to be stuck in the back room of the livery listening to special agents Barnes and Roper, not even bothering to pretend he cared about anything they might have to say.

"You need to hear this, Brand."

"So you bugged the brothel. Why should I care?"

"Shut up and listen," snapped Roper, the taller, meaner-looking one of the duo. He hit a button to fast-forward. The first taped voice Brand heard was male.

"I'm bringing in Mister X, Valerie. I'll need his special suite prepared."

Barnes paused the tape. "That's Lamoy. Valerie Lamoy is

his daughter. Heavy mob connections. He wants something here in Forked Creek. We haven't yet figured out what, but it's clear he won't rest till he has his hands on it. You don't want to be saying no to the higher-ups he answers to."

Brand didn't bother to share the fact that he'd already met Lamoy and knew exactly what the man was het up about.

The tape resumed with a woman's voice, sounding vexed. "I don't currently have anyone available for that specialty."

"Lamoy's daughter," Barnes identified, just as Lamoy's voice cut back in.

"You just get the room ready. I'll worry about the female companionship our distinguished guest requires."

"You know I've got a full house. What will the other guests think if they see you in the company of a minor?"

"I'll use the old tunnel. No one will even know she's on the premises. Except the one who matters, of course."

"That last tape wasn't good enough?"

"Can't ever have too much to work with when it comes to our influential friends, now, can we?"

"Is that why there's a new tape in the collection— Mitchell Brand and his consort out at the hot springs?"

"Insurance, my dear. Rainy day insurance."

Brand kept his face impassive, recalling how once or twice he'd caught a flash of reflected sunlight off in the distance. He'd thought it was just paranoia left over from the old days; seems he'd been wrong.

"So Lamoy's daughter has the shack wired for movies, does she? What do you want from me?"

"Nothing much," Barnes replied. "We figure you know

how to access the tunnel to get in and out of Madam Valerie's. Figured you might want to get your hands on the tape that has your special smile," he added with a smirk.

"And while you're in there," said Roper, "perhaps you'll spot something that will be of interest to us."

"I assume you gentlemen know who the mysterious Mr. X is?"

"Ninety percent. We need full confirmation."

"Why don't you two bust into Valerie's yourselves and snag my tape while you're at it. That way I'll owe you."

"Not our line of expertise, I'm afraid."

"Why should I care?"

"You probably don't, for yourself. But having your little librarian friend pop up on some porn channel could end her career."

"It's nothing to do with me."

"You used to have a soft spot for the underdog."

Used to being the key words; that had bought him nothing but grief. "No soft spots for any but number one these days."

Barnes cracked a rusty, seldom-used grimace that Brand suspected was supposed to be a smile. "You made it abundantly clear in your earlier career that you don't trust anyone to do the job right unless you do it yourself. We thought we'd offer you that opportunity for old times' sake."

"Mighty nice of you two fellows. Mighty nice."

PARIS LUXURIATED IN THE OLD-FASHIONED TUB of steaming water, determined never to take indoor plumbing for granted again. Even though her bath was nowhere as . . . stimulating as her soak in the hot springs, it felt divine.

She dipped the terry cloth and squeezed it across her shoulders, watching the slow trickle of warm water down her bare arm. She flexed her fingers and studied her hand as she recalled the intoxicating freedom of running her hands across Brand's chest, to tangle the masculine whorls of crisp chest hair beneath her touch.

Just the image of Brand sent remembered delight dancing through her limbs. She shifted in the tub and felt the tender pull at the juncture of her thighs. A rush of secret female satisfaction nested low in her belly. Insatiable! Getting back onto the horse afterward had been a challenge, yet a few hours later, she was primed to see Brand again.

She slid down to wet her hair, then shampooed it. The house had a dumbwaiter to make the servants' job easier as they hauled buckets of hot water and filled her tub. She dunked and rinsed, then applied conditioner, thankful for modern amenities. Everyone ought to spend a few days in Forked Creek, just to know how lucky they were.

She wondered how often Martha May managed to wash her hair, and how badly it tangled without the aid of modern hair products. She ran her Venus razor across her legs, checking her skin's smoothness with her free hand. Women wouldn't have bothered to shave their legs in Martha May's day. Perhaps life was simpler and easier. Then she thought about the risks: pregnancy, disease, how even something as simple as a bladder infection could prove deadly with no antibiotics. She definitely preferred life in the twenty-first century.

But she could get into the fun of role-playing while she had the chance. She clambered from the tub and toweled dry, running a hand through her hair to fluff it. Brand had told her to stay in her room till he arrived. Wouldn't it be fun if she managed to surprise him?

She rummaged in her bag for the bottle of chocolate body paint, courtesy Janine, pulled the cork, and smiled as she inhaled the unmistakable smell of Belgian chocolate. As she recorked it, she hoped it wouldn't clash with the sultry fragrance she had bought. She sprayed her upper body liberally with "Provocative Woman," then totally on impulse, spritzed the entrance of her female passage. Anticipation sparked a fresh flood of excitement as she attacked the closet till she found exactly what she was looking for: a cowgirl outfit the likes of which Brand had never seen before.

Buttery soft suede chaps, the color of nearly ripe wheat, matched a very skimpy bolero vest. Adding a cowboy hat, Paris posed in front of the cheval mirror, hardly able to believe her eyes. The vest barely covered her breasts, and was tied with a skinny lace that one halfhearted tug would undo.

Chaps, which she'd always found such a masculine piece of apparel, fueled all manner of fantasies. The suede molded her thighs like a second skin, then flared slightly from knee to ankle to take on a sassy life of their own every time she moved. She turned around, admiring the way the garment gloved her legs in back and exposed the perky cheeks of her bottom, still rosy from her bath. In the dim light it was difficult to tell where the suede ended and she began. She spun around. The flares flapped, the exposed V of her womanhood suggestively subtle. She cocked her head at an angle and imagined herself with a slim, pungent cigar dangling from her lips, maybe a holster and a six-shooter strapped to one leg. No one would mess around with her.

Except Brand. He would never be fooled by her "tough girl" look. Brand alone would know the way to her soft, vulnerable inner woman. His skill for touching her as no one ever had, both physically and emotionally, would have frightened her if it didn't feel so darn good.

Deep in her musings, she finally realized someone was knocking on her door.

"Paris, it's Brand. Are you in there?"

"Come in," she called as she dove for the bed and arranged herself in what she hoped was a sultry half recline, legs crossed at the ankle.

The door flew open and Brand was inside almost before the words had left her lips. "Come on," he said. "There's something I need to show you back at the hotel." He didn't even notice her getup.

"And there's something I need to show *you*. Right here," she added as she rose to stand before him. She held her breath. Never before had she been so daring; she would have been afraid of rejection or, worse yet, of scorn.

Clearly rejection was not an issue, judging by the utter amazement on his face and the way shock warred with lust. The intensity of his gaze seared right through her as she sashayed up to him with a suggestive sway to her hips and an unmistakable invitation on her lips.

"I've been waiting for you." She walked right into him till

their bodies collided and she rubbed herself against him. The cold silver of his belt buckle caught against her bare midriff. She heard him catch his breath, as she gave a tug to the lace fastening her vest.

He leaned down and kissed her, hard and hot and hungry, his tongue owning the inside of her mouth.

"You like the outfit?" she murmured against his lips.

"I *love* the outfit," he said. "Now throw a cloak over it and let's get out of here."

"What?" She took a step back. "What did you just say?" In her fantasy, Brand tossed her down on the bed and slowly nibbled her from head to toe, exploring and tasting every exposed inch of her.

In reality, he was riffling through the closet. He pulled out an ugly wool cloak that he bundled her into, pausing only long enough to grab a pair of shoes and her overnight bag.

"Would you mind telling me what this is all about?"

"All in good time," he said, then dropped his voice to a near whisper as he spoke directly into her ear. "Smile for the camera, Princess."

The meaning of his words, the reason for his behavior, hit like a thunderbolt. Her gaze casually swept the room. The ceiling? The mirror?

She swallowed mortification at the back of her throat, giggled, and leaned into Brand, tucking her arm through his. "You taking me away from this place, cowboy?"

"You bet your buckskins." Beneath the voluminous cloak, he gave her bare backside a sound slap for emphasis, then opened the door.

They were barely halfway down the staircase before Val's office door flew open. As the blonde watched their descent, the doorway behind her filled with the burly silhouette of a man in shadow.

"You taking my girl?" Val addressed Brand in a manner Paris suspected would do justice to the memory of Martha May herself.

Brand stepped easily into the assigned role. "Yes, ma'am."

"Overnights cost extra."

"I understand." Brand pulled out a roll of bills, peeled off a handful, and pressed them on Val. "This ought to cover it amply."

The shadow behind Val moved forward and Paris recognized the older man she had met earlier. He didn't spare Paris a glance; it was clearly Brand who held his interest.

"Well, well. Still here, are you?"

"For now," Brand said easily.

"How long you fetching to stay?"

"Not long."

"How long?"

"Long as a few things take to see themselves settled."

Luke appeared to take Brand's measure. If he was banking on intimidating the younger man, it wasn't working. He must have reached the same conclusion, for he hitched his belt, which rested just beneath his belly, and extended his hand. "Well, then, anything I can help you with, feel free to give a holler."

Brand took the man's proffered hand. "Mighty obliged to you. Now if you'll excuse us, I've got some special plans for this special lady over at my hotel."

"The place really is bugged," Paris said, once they were safely away from the bordello. "There was no other way for them to know we were on our way out. Is every room under surveillance or just mine?"

When Brand shrugged, Paris resisted the urge to stamp her feet in frustration. Obviously he knew a whole lot more than he was prepared to share. So much for all his talk earlier of pooling resources.

"How did you learn about the camera, anyway?"

"It's a long story, best saved for the hotel and a fortified beverage."

"You don't give away a lot, do you, Brand?"

"Princess, I don't give away a thing."

Chapter Nine

"*I don't like it,*" Luke said, staring at the front door as it closed behind Brand and Paris.

"Don't like what?" Valerie said, with only half her attention.

"That boy spells trouble."

"In what way?"

"He's got 'wild card' written all over him."

"You're paranoid," Valerie said. "He seems quite taken with Mistress Sommer, and she with him."

"You don't find that suspicious?"

"You think everything looks suspect."

"Usually because it is. Let me remind you, you're not running a dating agency, Valerie."

"I was under the impression I was running a historic tourist attraction."

"The house sits just outside of city limits, which makes it an ideal location for just about anything we want to do with it."

"'We' being you and your unsavory business associates."

"There's nothing unsavory about men making investments in the future of a place."

"The political figures you blackmail with the tapes from the rooms upstairs might think otherwise."

"Buyer beware," Luke said. "Are you keeping our fair mayor in line these days?"

"Don't I always do what I'm told, like a good little girl?"

"It'd be a sad day if a man couldn't trust his only daughter."

Princess, I don't give away a thing.

Brand wondered if Paris knew how those terse words revealed everything about him.

Sweet Paris, with no clue as to the challenge she posed. When he'd burst into her room tonight and caught sight of her in that outfit, he thought he'd expire from the overwhelming intensity of it, the fact that she could be so playful. The prim librarian had been left behind in Seattle, her place taken by this spunky, risk-taking, fun-loving sexpot.

He'd craved nothing more than to tumble her to the bed, to bury his face between those suede-encased thighs and make her scream and arch up with pleasure beneath him. Wouldn't that make some interesting viewing for the Lamoys? Except Brand planned to be long gone by the time the duo discovered what was missing, along with a few select tapes from their video blackmail library.

Neither he nor Paris spoke again until the privacy of his hotel room, where Paris paced in circles and clung to the cloak, her earlier playfulness gone.

"How do you know this room isn't bugged as well?"

He'd given it a thorough sweep, but he didn't want to get into the hows and whys of his background with the secret service.

"Trust me, it's clean."

She halted and turned to face him. "You haven't exactly said or done a whole lot to gain a girl's trust, Brand."

"I thought trust was given."

"I believe trust has to be earned."

Stalemate. "Speaking of trust." He opened a bureau drawer and passed her the journal. "Missing this?"

She grabbed the book as if it were a newborn child and hugged it to her chest. "Where did you . . . ?"

"Obviously Lamoy or one of his cronies helped themselves. I simply stole it back. Thought you might need it."

He watched the way uncertainty tinged the mossy depths of her eyes. "How do I know you didn't take it in the first place, then claim someone else did, trying to make yourself look good?"

"Because I don't give a damn about looking good. Not to you or anyone else. But if I had been the one to steal it, I'd have been mighty pissed."

"What do you mean?"

"All this talk about a treasure map, and there's no map anywhere in the book. Or is the map someplace safe back in Seattle?"

She watched him closely. "They must have known where I hid the journal in my room because of the hidden camera."

"Bingo! Now what's the bullshit about a map?"

She slumped down onto the edge of the bed. "Why should I tell you?"

"It's completely up to you. But whatever you're looking for, you're not doing such a great job of it on your own." And if by some weird fluke she led the way to that missing deed Warren wanted, he could clear out of here with a clean conscience.

He watched the way she weighed her options as the cloak slowly slid from her shoulders, which he took as a sign of surrender and reacted accordingly. He knelt in front of her, put his hands on her knees, and coaxed them apart.

"I didn't get a chance earlier to express my wholehearted approval of your costume."

"You can't just change the subject like that. We're in the middle of something important here."

"Uh-uh," he said. "We're on the cusp of starting something extremely important."

A band of skin a shade or two paler than the revealing suede chaps invited him closer. He traced the crease at the top of her thigh with his finger and wondered how anyone could have such soft, soft skin.

"How did you feel when you were getting dressed, getting ready to see me tonight?"

Her legs relaxed and slowly parted, affording him a moist

pink glimmer of the delights within, like petals of a dew-kissed rose, darker at the center.

"Did you feel sexy? Did you get excited?"

Her lids lowered till her eyes were provocatively half shut. He doubted she was even aware of her own actions as she outlined her lips with the tip of her tongue and made them glisten moistly in the pale gaslight. Her lips deepened in color, much like the other lips that peeked shyly at him from between her legs.

Which lips were most deserving of his first attentions? It was a difficult call.

"I felt sexy and daring. More daring than I've ever been in my life."

"I like you daring. Did you get excited?"

She nodded dreamily.

"Did you get wet?"

She pinkened slightly and gave him an enticing, secret smile—the smile of a woman who has recently discovered the full power of her sexuality. "Yes." Her voice was so sexy-husky it was almost his undoing.

"Did you touch yourself? Pretend it was me?"

"No," she said. "I wanted to wait for you."

He gently teased the triangle of curls, absorbing their springy moisture before he grazed them lightly with the back of his fingers.

"Good thing you didn't start without me. Old Luke would likely have got himself off watching."

She shuddered. "I don't think I can go back there, knowing I'm being watched."

Damn, he'd gone and spoiled the mood. She'd lost that dreamy, heavy-lidded, half-aroused look. "How did you know about the camera?" she asked.

"I know Lamoy's reputation."

"You're a complicated man, Mitchell Brand the third. I know you have your own agenda for being here."

"Here with you? Or here in Forked Creek?"

"Both, I suspect." She flopped back on the bed. "Why are things suddenly so complicated? This trip was supposed to be a fun little romp for me—an adventure. I've not had many of those."

"Well, then, Princess, let me see what I can do to make this time between us a totally fun adventure."

"I thought you wanted to pool our resources."

He levered himself over her, weight on his arms, and lowered his lips to her exposed midriff. "I'd say that's exactly what we're doing."

At the first pass with his tongue, she tensed. He felt her abs contract sharply, then slowly relax as he nipped the soft skin near her navel, drawing circles around it before he gave it a gentle suck. She quivered slightly and was still as he traced a lazy pathway lower, over the waist ties of the chaps, past her pubic bone, to dip into the sweetest part of her.

He lifted her legs up to straddle his shoulders and she opened herself wide to him. The cosmetics industry knew what it was doing when it created the colors for women's lips. He paused for a second to look his fill, from the luscious plump outer lips, where pale pink tones deepened to hotter pink, nearly red inner lips engorged with blood, swollen and hot—as hot as the woman herself. He blew lightly, teased her with the lightest of caresses.

She murmured and shifted her hips in invitation, luring him in deeper, closer, like a Siren luring a vessel's captain to imminent disaster on a hidden reef.

The immediate danger was that Brand found himself starting to care what happened to Paris, as something long frozen inside of him—something he thought had passed from his life along with his father—sparked long-forgotten feelings.

Feelings he effectively squelched as he clamped his hands on Paris's thighs and pushed her legs farther apart. He scooped her by her bottom to raise her hips off the bed. He could take her now. Drive himself into her hard and fast and forever banish those uncomfortable feelings from his life.

Or he could proceed slowly, pleasure her the way she deserved, and risk turning into a caring, feeling individual. It wasn't a comfortable thought, and as he weighed his options, Paris decided for him.

First she unfastened her vest to expose the enticing domes of her breasts. Lovingly she touched them, urging the perky nipples to stand at attention, perfectly formed rosebuds savoring the stimulating warmth of human touch.

From her breasts she slid her hands over her rib cage to her abdomen, then lower, to the secret, vulnerable inner core exposed only to him. She trailed her hands along the soft skin of her inner thighs, clasped them gently, then shyly touched herself.

Brand gently stroked her ass, encouraging her to continue, unable to tear his gaze from the tableau before him.

Boldly she dipped her middle finger into the moist, glistening slit and separated the hidden folds of her inner tabernacle. Her finger was damp from her own juices as she circled the entryway.

He could see the tip of her clit peeking shyly from its hood, then slowly blossom to full bloom as she lightly grazed it with one fingertip.

Daintily she dipped her finger inside, then dragged it up over her clit, only to sink it back deep inside herself.

He continued to fondle the globes of her ass as she increased the pace at which she alternately stroked and entered, withdrew and stroked. His cock strained against the fly of his jeans. The room was silent save the rise and fall of his harshly indrawn breath. Or was that hers?

Her eyes were shut, her free hand caressing her round ripe nipples. She was streaming wet and her fingers glistened with the moisture of desire. He knew she'd feel divine, hot and wet and tight. And soon he'd have her. But not yet.

He popped his baby finger into his mouth to dampen it, then massaged the opening of her anus till he felt it soften and give way beneath his touch. Slowly, carefully, so as not to hurt her, he slipped his pinkie in, then out, then back in. The pace at which she rubbed herself escalated with his. Her breath flowed in shallow pants. Her entire vulva was flushed red, more beautiful than the most perfect red rose.

He felt her sphincter tighten around his baby finger as the first wave of orgasmic pleasure shuddered through her. Her back arched and her eyes fastened on his as her entire body shuddered with the force of her release.

As she sagged back down against him on the bed, he gently pulled his hands out from underneath her. He stroked the slackness of her relaxed thigh muscles, gentling her as she exhaled a sigh of pure carnal pleasure.

When he pressed a kiss to those luscious inner petals and delicately sipped at the ripples of delicious aftershocks, the sweetness of her sent a jolt of desire coursing through him.

Unable to resist a quick sip, he dipped his tongue into that honeyed inner sanctum. To his utter amazement she moved against him, with him, amidst soft murmurs of encouragement.

He shifted his angle of approach to increase the pressure of his lips and his tongue as he worshiped her, thanking her for the special gift she had just bestowed upon him.

Mild aftershocks quickly grew to become full-blown fall-outs as her body responded to his and Paris gave herself over to him totally, flooding into him through his lips. As she moaned and sighed her way through several more orgasms Brand knew he couldn't wait much longer.

He repositioned her higher on the bed, knees bent, and skinned out of his jeans. He straddled her and rubbed her all over with his impatient cock, pausing to play with her breasts, tickle her navel, then slip his aching hardness between her eagerly awaiting lips. Lovingly she tongued him and he nearly went out of his mind. He pulled back and pressed a fervent kiss to her lips, drawing more of her essence into him before he buried himself inside her.

Her guttural moan of delight was music to him as he threaded his fingers through her hair and rode her hard and fast.

She gloved him, melting around him, her muscles alternately slack and giving, finally hugging him so tight he could barely move. He felt the start of another orgasm for her and with a cry of surrender, he gave himself over to the pleasure of release. Deep, intense, his climax seemed to go on forever, seconded by hers, milking every last drop from him.

Paris didn't know how long they lay there like that in a tangle of sweat-dewed limbs as she gently stroked his back and felt the way his heart thudded against hers.

She'd never behaved so outrageously before in her life. Even more startling, she liked this new side of her. She had Brand to thank for bringing out a part of herself she hadn't even known existed. A part of her that was more real than all those years she'd spent trying to be "Perfect Paris." Finally she'd discovered her true spirit, the most important part of who she really was.

Suddenly, through the fog of sexual satiation, she became aware of a ruckus somewhere beyond the room. She heard raised voices, a gunshot, more shouting, followed by the sound of footfalls in the hall.

Brand leaped to the window with Paris right behind him. "What is it? What's going on?" she asked.

Below them on the street, she saw the beginnings of a crowd milling about, then slowly moving together as they hugged the sidewalk. One man stood alone in the middle of the street, staggering in an ever-widening circle, gun pointed skyward, yelling something unintelligible.

"Could be nothing," Brand muttered. But he stepped into his jeans as he spoke.

"Wait for me." Paris quickly dressed in the first thing at hand from her bag—cargo shorts and a baby T—then followed him from the hotel to the street.

The man who appeared to have started the uproar was no longer alone. He had been joined by a second man, each of whom was gesturing threateningly toward the other.

"Do you think it's staged?" Paris asked, knowing even as she spoke that it wasn't. There was a hushed, heavy atmosphere in the street, nothing like the lighthearted fun of the shooting gallery. People were sidling into doorways to take cover before they peered out cautiously to see what was going on.

"Hard to say. Stay in back of the crowd, just in case." Then he turned and melted through the onlookers.

Brand made his way to where Barnes and Roper stood in a shadowy doorway in deep debate. If anyone was in the know, it would be those two.

"Well?" he demanded.

"Word on the street is someone got caught with their pants down in the wrong woman's bed. Joe's calling for a shoot-out."

The two men were still gesturing wildly toward each other.

"Aren't those two of Lamoy's goons?"

"Yep. They're serious and their guns are loaded. We need to put a stop to this."

"It's likely a setup," Brand said. "Lamoy's attempt to flush you two out into the open. He knows if you're nearby you won't be able to sit still for this."

"Then he knows right," Barnes said.

"Sit tight," Brand said. "We'll spike his guns. I'll deal with those two hotheads. Don't step in unless it becomes absolutely necessary."

"Since when have you been a team player?" said Roper.

"Or a hero?" said Barnes.

"Gentlemen, you don't know me at all."

From her vantage point, Paris watched in horror as the two armed men turned back to back in the center of the street and began to count out their paces, like something from a bad spaghetti Western. Her horror was doubly compounded when Brand stepped directly between them.

What on earth was he doing?

She stuffed her fist into her mouth. What could she do? From the abundance of threatening gestures and off-color language, she could tell neither man was the least bit interested in listening to Brand.

She clenched her fingers together. Suddenly there was a buzz of surprise from those watching as a second man joined Brand and allied himself against the two hotheads.

Chapter Ten

"*What the hell do you think you're doing?*" Brand asked Warren.

"Saving your sorry hide one more time."

"Didn't know you thought it was even worth saving."

"You've overlooked one important detail: you haven't completed the little task I assigned you."

"Get out of here before you get hurt." Brand's tone said that the real threat was not the two lunatics they were faced off against.

A threat Warren chose to disregard. "There's safety in numbers. Those clowns are unlikely to do anything stupid now that there's two of us."

Where the hell were you when we were growing up?
Brand wondered.

More men arrived, following Warren's example, creating
a human blockade between the two hotheads. Before long
the duo gave up in disgust, holstered their weapons, and
stomped off in opposite directions.

A collective sigh ran through the onlookers, followed by a
buzz of conversation. Cynically, Brand figured most of them
were disappointed by the anti-climactic conclusion.

At least Barnes and Roper hadn't needed to blow their
cover, if that had indeed been the reason for the set-to.

The tension at the back of his neck begin to subside as
Barnes and Roper melted into the shadows. Brand glanced
toward the hotel. Best collect Paris and head back there; he
didn't like leaving the journal lying around. It wouldn't be
long before the Lamoys discovered it had been reclaimed,
along with the tape he'd delivered earlier to Barnes and
Roper. The Lamoys had a nice little extortion racket going,
which Warren would be mighty pissed about. He considered
Forked Creek his town, and pure as the fresh-driven snow.

"Think they'll try it again?" Warren asked.

"Nah. They'll more than likely forget all about it by
morning."

Slowly the crowd began to disperse. Brand left, and Warren watched him make his way back to Paris's side.

"To what do we owe that foolish show of bravado?"

The scorn in Warren's mother's voice was an ever-present
part of her. Nothing he ever did was good enough, fast
enough, smart enough. And never would be.

"I couldn't let Brand look like a hero all by himself, could I?"

"I warned you before about allying yourself with those Brands."

She seemed to forget that she was the one who had connected them both with the Brand family in the first place. "Yes, Mother. You've spent a lifetime telling me what to do and how to act."

"Then get on with it," the old lady hissed.

She turned about smartly and left him standing in the middle of the now-deserted dark street. This town, his legacy, was proving to be both a curse and a blessing. He was proud to be part of a dream first realized by his father and his grandfather, but his mother's constant interference, along with the shareholders' continual harpings about expansion and profit-and-loss statements, were enough to exhaust even the most resilient of men.

Time was running out. Was he wrong to count on Brand to come up with the missing deed to the bordello? His stepbrother was well known for always having his own agenda. If he couldn't count on himself and he couldn't count on Brand, who could he count on? Slowly Warren turned and found his way to the one place he knew he would be safe.

Val opened the door herself. "Warren, sweetheart. I just heard about the incredibly brave thing you did!"

"It wasn't so much." He walked directly into her arms and pulled her close. "I need you, Val."

"Of course you do," she said soothingly. "Let's go upstairs to my room."

Inside Val's room, Warren got a towel and spread it on the bed. Then he removed his pants and lay face down across the towel. Behind him, he heard Val's approach.

"You've been a very naughty boy, Warren."

"Yes, Mother," he mumbled into the mattress.

"You know what happens to bad little boys, don't you?"

"Yes, Mother." Warren flinched at the first mild slap of her bare hand across his buttocks. Gradually the slaps became more forceful, stinging his buttocks and the backs of his legs. He felt himself grow harder with each subsequent blow, especially when her wooden hair brush replaced her hand. Minutes later, he had spent himself on the towel.

"Roll over, you naughty boy. Let Mommy look at the mess you've made."

Obediently Warren rolled over, avoiding his sticky ejaculate. Val hiked her skirt up around her waist and lowered herself onto his face. "Now show Mommy just how much you love her."

PARIS DIDN'T KNOW IF SHE OUGHT TO HUG Brand or to shake him. "Did it ever occur to you what an incredibly foolish thing that was to do?"

"They were too cowardly to go through with it. They just needed to save face," Brand said.

"Who was that second man who joined you? He looked familiar."

"That was Warren West. His family were the original founders of Forked Creek, and later generations spearheaded the restoration. Poor bastard."

"Why do you say that? I would think it's a wonderful thing to be part of."

"He grew up knowing this town was his legacy, and too damn bad if he didn't wish to take it on."

"Do you think he resents it?"

"I don't think he thinks about it one way or the other. He does what he's told."

"I wonder if someone told him to ignore my calls or to discourage my visit," Paris said. "I met him at Val's the other night and he wasn't overly pleased to learn I was here. Maybe he likes to have an exclusive on the family connection."

Brand shrugged. "The Wests have always been superterritorial."

"Territorial" perfectly described the way Brand was eyeing her right now. "I guess I should think about heading back to the bordello." Paris was feeling suddenly unaccountably shy. Was it because she was in her own clothes?

"What's your rush?"

"There is that dumb curfew."

"There're ways around that. Now, where were we when we were so rudely interrupted?"

"If I recall correctly, we were basking in the afterglow."

"That's right," Brand said. "Which means we have to start from scratch again."

Every drop of estrogen in her body leaped to attention in keen agreement. When he took her in his arms, she decided that treasure hunting would be more productive in the daylight anyway.

He kissed her hard with a hungry greed she responded

hesitantly to. She'd been wild earlier, totally out of character. Now she was afraid of disappointing him—worse yet, disappointing herself.

"What happened to my cowgirl?" he asked huskily, toying with the fastening of her cargo shorts. Brand must have sensed the change in her kiss, felt her tentativeness. His knuckles grazed the skin near her waist and she felt herself begin to melt. His touch was magic. Brand magic.

"I'm not sure. It's easy to be less inhibited when I'm in costume, pretending to be someone else."

"I like you being just exactly who you are," Brand said, as he continued to stroke her midriff.

No one had ever told her that before, but his words didn't still her butterflies. Her mouth felt dry. Why was she so suddenly nervous? This was far from their first time together, yet in some ways it felt like the first. Had the others been merely practice for the real thing? The gradual letting down of all her guard, till there was nothing left to hold back?

"No one knows who I really am," she said. "I change all the time to try and meet people's expectations."

"I have no expectations. So how about we just play it as it comes?"

Paris gnawed her lower lip. If only it was so easy. "I don't know how to play. I only know how to playact."

"You and me earlier was no act; that was totally real. Every time we've been together, it's been real. Something solid and rare enough that it's worth hanging on to with both hands."

How badly she wanted to believe him. She also wanted to

be who he wanted her to be—sexy and wild and uninhibited. He spoke of hanging on, as if their time together was more than just a seize-the-moment opportunity.

She sighed. Why couldn't she be more spontaneous? Why was she cursed with an analytical mind that weighed and measured every nuance and identified Brand as a calculated risk factor that sent her into panic mode even as it made him impossible to resist?

And really, why should she even try to resist him? "I'll try and learn to play if you will."

"You don't think I'm a playful guy?"

"I think deep down you're a lot more like me than you let on. That's why we connect."

He stiffened, as if she'd gotten a little too close. "I'm responsible only to and for myself. That's the way it's always been. That's the way I like it."

Listen to us, Paris thought. Two loners trying to pretend we deliberately chose to be that way when really all we did was play the hand we were dealt.

"I think," she said with a playful purr, "that it's time for a little dessert."

From her bag she pulled the bottle of chocolate body paint. "Do you have a sweet tooth?"

Brand eyed her hungrily. "I do if it includes you."

Paris pulled the cork and dipped the paintbrush inside. It came out covered in liquid, gooey chocolate. Impulsively, she painted a thick, dark chocolate mustache on Brand's upper lip. He stuck out his tongue and tasted it. "Belgian, if I'm not mistaken."

"My favorite." They leaned forward together, but instead of kissing her, he rubbed his chocolate mustache all over her face, which gave him the excuse to lick it off. Then he nipped at her breasts, sucked them through the thin cotton of her T-shirt, and left the front of her shirt streaked with chocolate residue.

"Now your shirt's all dirty," he said huskily. "Better take it off."

"All in good time." Nimbly she unfastened the pearl buttons fronting his denim shirt, then pushed it aside to reveal his lean chest and torso. "I think you need a tattoo." She painted a heart near his collarbone.

"Marking your territory?"

"Perhaps." She added a cupid's arrow through the heart. If only it was so simple to mark Brand as hers.

"Here." He took the paintbrush from her hand and pushed her shirt out of the way to bare her shoulder. "A butterfly," he said. She felt the cool, gooey chocolate, the sweep of bristles across her skin, followed by the warm, sinewy pathway of his tongue as he licked her clean.

"You taste delicious. Yum, yum." She felt the gentle nip of his teeth against her skin, his mouth and lips moving in ever-widening hungry circles. Did he know the power he had to consume her completely?

He slid his hands around her waist and drew her back against him as he tossed her shirt onto the floor. He reached around and painted her breasts, outlining the areola, the wet stimulation of the brush pebbling her nipples.

She leaned against him, eyes closed, and surrendered to

the heat of his breath against her neck, to his hungry, devouring tongue, and the way his clever hands shaped the softness of her breasts.

He lowered her to the bed, tugged off her shorts, and stepped from his jeans to straddle her, his hard cock primed toward her.

He pushed her chocolate-covered breasts together and slid his cock into the valley between them, using the chocolate paint to ease the in-out glide.

Paris grew unbearably excited as she watched him pump between her breasts, laving them both in chocolaty goodness as he teased her nipples.

"I need a taste." She opened her mouth.

He edged forward and outlined her lips with the tip of his chocolate-covered cock. "Sweets for the sweet."

The smooth, sweet chocolate was a distinct contrast to Brand's salty-musky taste, flooding her with fresh longing. She eased him all the way into her mouth, ran her tongue over his length, and commenced to suck him greedily.

Soon he pulled his cock from her mouth, then leaned over to lick her clean. From there he kissed his way down her body, first between her breasts, then down to sample her navel, her hip bones, and the tops of her legs.

The brush tickled as he drew a line of chocolate paint down her body, fashioning a sassy daisy on the inside of one thigh and a smiling sun on the other.

Finally he poured some liquid chocolate into the palm of his hand and anointed her female chalice.

"That's cold." Paris shivered.

"Only because you're so hot. And I'm going to make you boil."

"That brings new meaning to the term 'hot chocolate.'" Paris grinned.

"You're hot chocolate." He slid two fingers inside of her and drew them out, dripping with chocolate and female desire. He popped them into his mouth.

"Delicious." He leaned forward and offered her a taste of one. She pulled his finger deep into her mouth as he inserted his other hand inside of her, then withdrew. Insert. Shallow. Deep.

Hips bucking, she sucked his fingers in time to his thrusts.

When his thumb grazed her clit, she felt herself spasm and she cried out in release. Brand pushed her breasts back together and buried himself in the snug chocolate sheath, pumping her with equal abandon. Seconds later his semen spurted across her breasts, turning the Belgian chocolate into a milk chocolate bath for the two of them.

PARIS PAGED THROUGH THE BRITTLE, yellowed pages of Martha May's journal, a shudder of distaste running through her at the thought of Lamoy's sweaty hands violating her book. How dare he? If not for Brand, the book would no longer be in her possession. Although she'd committed the clues in the map to memory, the book meant more to her than any elusive treasure. It was a tangible link to her past, hidden clues to her genetic makeup. Perhaps even reasons for some of the pathways she'd chosen in her life.

At this point in her life the most surprising of choices was her decision to trust Brand, for she'd decided to enlist his help in seeking out Martha May's hidden treasure. She, who was used to going it alone, was about to do something totally out of character, something that would leave her wide open and vulnerable on every level. She could weigh the individual factors forever, but in the end it came down to instinct. Her need to trust Brand was greater than her need to hang on to her independence at all costs.

"Do you think Luke could have had the journal copied?"

"Doubtful. There's no photocopier in Forked Creek."

"Do you think he even looked at it?"

"I expect he pawed through and tossed it aside in disgust when there was no map."

"Things are not always as they seem, you know."

"Are you going to explain that cryptic sentence?"

"Martha May's journal contains a map of words. Every few pages, a phrase is printed instead of written. There was lots of double-dealing and intrigue in the town in those days, and Martha May was in the thick of it. Not only that, people trusted her.

"Specifically, Otis trusted her. Do you really think it's a coincidence that those grave robbers were digging up his grave? There's something . . . I don't know what it is, but maybe something disappeared years ago, entrusted to Martha May for safekeeping. And the map is the key to finding it."

"And you believe that now, all these years later, a random group of people are dashing around all seeking the same prize?"

"You needn't make it sound so implausible." Paris picked up the book to leave. So much for baring her soul and her secrets. She ought to have known Brand would laugh.

"Hey!" His hands atop hers stilled her. "That's not my intent. Quite the opposite. Show me how we get started."

Paris studied his face, dark and dangerous, crowned by sexily rumpled hair against the pristine white bed linen. He sounded sincere. But didn't men often say one thing and think another? Did the fact that they were good in bed together—no, stupendous in bed together—mean they'd be a good team in other ways, or was she setting herself up for a major disappointment?

He sat there watching her in a way that made her wonder if her thoughts were transparent.

"Unless you don't want my help."

Paris sighed. Now he sounded hurt. "It's the sex," she blurted out.

He looked surprised. "What about it?"

"It just . . . Just because we've been close in that way, it doesn't necessarily mean that things will work out if we get close in other ways."

"Come here." He pulled her against him, tightly in the sheltering circle of his arms. "Did someone love you and leave you?"

Yes, I was jilted at the altar. But she still couldn't bring herself to say the words out loud. All she knew was that no one had ever loved her with the depth and intensity that she needed, that she was capable of returning. And because she was afraid of getting hurt in the bargain, she'd become an expert at holding back. How had Brand stepped over those boundaries as if they didn't exist, as if he knew her better than she knew herself?

Or had he just held up the mirror through which she viewed herself? She didn't want to rely on Brand, allow him to be the conduit through which she finally recognized and acknowledged who she was. And now, having finally discovered Paris—the real Paris—could she afford to lose herself immediately, to Brand?

There she went, overanalyzing again, when she ought to just enjoy this adventure, make the most of it in every possible way, and then return to her life with no regrets.

She pulled up the journal and opened its faded, cracked cover. Snugged against Brand, feeling his skin warm hers, she felt protected and cared for as she leafed through the pages. She knew all the significant passages by heart, and paused to read aloud paragraphs that might be significant. Once she pointed out the pattern of the word map, Brand seemed to catch on quickly. He produced paper and pen and wrote down the key words.

When they were done, they had a list that consisted of:

Hope Springs Eternal
Untapped Riches
Cast-off Temptation
The Sins of the Flesh
Forever Among Us
Renewal of Life

"'Hope Springs Eternal.'" Brand underlined the word *springs*. "That's why you were up at the hot springs. What did you find up there?"

"Some carvings in the rocks."

"What kind of carvings?"

"I think it was a date, along with a triangle and a cross."

"A cross?" Brand asked.

"I don't think Martha May was particularly religious. The cross could be the cemetery."

He nodded. "Maybe someone else thinks so, too. Which could be why someone decided to dig up Otis's grave."

Chapter Eleven

Val nearly laughed out loud at the way Elspeth leaned on her ever-present cane and clung to the handrail as she slowly climbed up the front steps of the bordello. The old crow was no more frail than Val was, the ornate silver-headed cane nothing but a prop.

Elspeth didn't bother to knock, she simply entered as if she owned the place, which Val knew she was burning to do. Then she followed Val and her father to the front parlor.

"Where is it?" she demanded, forgoing all social niceties and chitchat. Val shot her father a look intended to display her disapproval. Ever the diplomat, her father had gone along with Elspeth's insistence that she be kept informed and updated about the retrieval of the journal and treasure map. Her father had enjoyed lording it over Elspeth when they'd gotten possession of the journal ahead of her.

"All in good time," Luke said, smoothly. "I haven't had the opportunity to get it authenticated, but I can tell you this: there is no map drawn anywhere in that book."

"What did you say?" Elspeth froze. "Incompetents. There has to be a map. We know that wretched woman squirreled away the deed before she ran off, and her book is the only link to finding it. Let me see it." She tapped the floor impatiently with her cane.

Luke wore a Cheshire cat grin. "Show Elspeth the book, Valerie."

Val removed a portrait of Martha May from the far wall to reveal the safe behind it, dismantled the hidden alarm, and unlocked it. The door swung open silently and Val reached inside, only to come up empty-handed. She dug about in vain, unable to credit the mockingly empty spot where the book had been earlier.

"There's no point in stalling, my dear. Be a good little girl and do as your daddy says."

Val ignored Elspeth's unpleasant chirping voice behind her as she took a quick inventory to see what else was missing. As far as she could tell, the stocks, cash, and jewelry were all intact, which made no sense.

She turned to face the other two. "It's not in here."

Elspeth gave a shriek of disbelief, while her father's face

darkened with displeasure. He rose, pushed her aside, and began to paw through the safe's contents.

"Don't take my word for it," Val said sarcastically. "See for yourself."

"How could that happen?" Elspeth turned accusing eyes on Luke. "You assured me it was safe here."

"It's simply not possible. Unless there's something my daughter has failed to tell me. You and Warren wouldn't be ganging up against us old folks, now, would you?"

"I learned about loyalty from the best," Val said sullenly.

"We're blood, you and me. Blood takes all."

"Except when dictated otherwise by your bosses. You do what they say regardless of my wishes."

"This house is useful to them, as well as to us. It's a shame if you have other ideas."

"I always have other ideas," Val said. "Not that you'll ever listen."

Luke's hand clenched into a fist at his side and Val knew she'd pushed him far enough. Nothing would ever be resolved between them; he was simply a puppet for those other men. Men who scared her because she knew they were capable of anything.

"No one else in town knows the value of that book," she said.

Elspeth's face grew pinched. "Mitchell Brand. I told Warren not to get him involved. That boy always was trouble."

"I doubt Brand had anything to do with the missing journal," Luke said.

Elspeth rose and faced him. "No doubt that's exactly what he wants you to think." She leveled a scrawny finger at Luke's chest. "Mark my words. You've got a far more serious problem on your hands than the book being missing."

"Seems to me it's your problem. It's your boy who brought him in."

"Mitchell Brand is everyone's problem. And don't dare to think otherwise."

Elspeth stomped from the room. Seconds later the front door slammed behind her, and Val faced her father. "Now what do we do?"

"We turn this town upside down until we get our hands on that book."

"But you said yourself there's no map."

"Maybe it's time we had a little chat with Miss Sommer. No, I've got an even better idea."

THE HONEYCOMB OF BELOWGROUND tunnels seemed smaller than in Brand's memory. They ran from the bordello at one end of town to the church at the other end, with side branches to the hotel, the saloon, and other key destinations.

As youngsters, Brand and Warren had been forbidden to play in them, which had only heightened their appeal. Forked Creek had historically been a stopping-off place for men on both sides of the law and the tunnels provided easy access to the town's amenities while allowing certain visitors not to be seen on the streets. They'd been well maintained as part of the restoration. Maybe one day they'd be on the guided tour.

Brand knew Lamoy had summoned him to this meeting to get the journal back, and he'd agreed to meet Lamoy directly below the hotel so he could be back in bed next to Paris before she even noticed his absence.

"If you've seen the book firsthand, you know there's no treasure map. Nothing even close. And I'm damn certain your boys didn't find anything in Otis's grave," he told Lamoy.

"Funny thing about that," Lamoy said. "Darn thing disappeared before I could make a complete study of it. Now, you're my kind of man. You see an opportunity and you take full advantage of it. And I'm about to offer you the opportunity of a lifetime."

"What makes you think I'd be interested?"

"Oh, you'll be interested, all right. My partners have deep pockets, and a very long memory for those who do right by us. I know you owe no loyalty to that stepbrother of yours and his witch of a mother. So ally yourself with the winning team."

"I'm all ears and empty pockets," Brand said.

BRAND WOKE PARIS BEFORE THE SUN had lightened the night sky. Half asleep, she shuffled downstairs with him and onto a stagecoach headed for The Outpost to pick up supplies. If Forked Creek was an authentically restored piece of history, The Outpost was its polar opposite, garish and touristy, fully commercialized. It boasted a bus depot and a train station, and after only a few minutes to see the journal safely secreted in a locker, they were back in the coach. With luck they'd be back in town before anyone even knew they had left. Paris stifled a yawn. Somehow, around Brand, there always seemed to be more interesting things to do than sleep.

"I don't feel good about leaving the journal there," she said wistfully. "I feel like I'm leaving part of myself behind."

"It's just for a few days. There's no place in Forked Creek you could stash it and feel secure."

"I know," Paris said. "It's just funny how you can get attached to things and feel lost without them." Or people. But there was no point letting Brand know she was in danger of becoming attached to him.

A fact that wasn't even scary. In the past, anytime she'd allowed herself to need a man it had ended badly and Paris was no fool. She knew the second that she felt the need of someone in her life, she felt weakened, which she overcompensated for by setting out to prove she needed no one. It was an effective way of scaring people from her life, perpetuating her role as a loner. Until Joel. And that had ended worse than anything she could have imagined. To stand at the altar and hear him announce that he was no longer prepared to marry her, that he had made a mistake . . .

The stagecoach hit a pothole, hurtling her against Brand, who caught and held her steady. She could feel the warmth of his touch through the sleeves of the denim jacket he had insisted on lending her. She loved the fact that it smelled exactly like him—outdoorsy, masculine, and spicy.

"Imagine when this was the only way to travel," he said.

"It's not exactly luxurious." The seats were hard; foam rubber had yet to be invented.

"It beat the saddle for long trips."

"Admit it. You'd pick the saddle any day," Paris said teasingly.

"Under normal circumstances, yes. But I can also see definite advantage to stage travel."

"Such as?"

"Here we are, with this rather boring journey ahead of us. What might we possibly do to while away the time?"

The coach swayed from side to side, flinging them atop each other as if in silent answer to his question.

"I didn't bring anything to read," Paris said. She felt a resurgence of faint female stirring from her nether regions. Would she ever get enough of this man?

"And I fear I neglected to bring along a deck of cards," Brand said.

"That does limit our options somewhat." Paris pretended to ponder. "What about a game of 'I Spy'?"

Brand leaned in close. "I spy with my little eye . . . something brown. Something small and soft and round."

"Is it in the coach?" Paris asked.

"I'm looking at it right now."

"I don't see anything like you just described."

He rested his hand on the side of her neck. "I'm touching it right now." He replaced his hand with his lips. "I'm kissing it right now," he murmured. "It's this tiny, soft, velvety mole." He nibbled lightly, then tongued the delicate dip between her collarbone and neck.

Paris leaned back, her eyes closed, awash in the rush of sensation. He knew her body like a road map of erogenous zones, as if their spirits were old acquaintances who recognized each other instantly. She could find no other explanation for this magic current that flowed between them. The pull that had been there from the very start grew stronger with every moment spent in his company.

Brand had recognized the true her. He'd stripped away the facade of "Perfect Paris" as effectively as he stripped off her garments, and both sensations were scary yet exhilarating, leaving her hungry for more.

He pulled her onto his lap so she straddled him as he buried his head between her breasts and drew a long, deep breath. Paris felt as if he were inhaling the very essence of her, drawing the heat and fire of her womanhood from her central core before he coaxed it to flow through her veins, to swell and overflow as it spilled through her, engulfing them both.

He hadn't shaved yet and she could feel the tickle of his overnight beard.

"I love the way you smell. I could drink it forever."

Paris's breath caught. The forever word. Far too dangerous for her vocabulary.

"Open your shirt. I want to taste your breasts. I need to feel your skin against mine."

Paris didn't require a second invitation. "I love the way you make me feel."

"What way is that?" His words were muffled as he busily drew tiny patterns on her cleavage with his tongue.

"You make me feel sexy. Desirable. Wantonly female."

"Feel what you do to me." He guided her hand to that blatantly male part of him, swollen against the zipper of his jeans. She followed the seam of his jeans and cupped the heavy heat of his package. As he took her breasts into his mouth and suckled, she felt an answering pull from deep within. Like a river lazily overflowing its banks, she felt the slow rise of pressure that started at the juncture of her legs and traveled both north and south, a warm, radiant outpouring of needful desire.

She slid off Brand's lap and opened his jeans. His impressive cock rose up to greet her like an old and welcome friend. She made a loose fist to ring his girth, and slowly slid her palm down his length. So hard and yet so soft. Velvety tip. Ramrod shaft. Nerve endings she'd never known she possessed in the palm of her hand sprang to life.

A bead of moisture bloomed at his tip and she dipped her head to whisk it away with her tongue, drinking in the salty-sweet taste of him as she inhaled the male musky odor of primitive, untamed man. It surrounded her, engulfed her, saturated her.

"These seem to be in the way."

When she tugged at his jeans, he obligingly raised his hips. "I quite agree."

As she lowered his jeans he did his part to kick them aside. She leaned forward, licked her lips in anticipation, and slowly slid his velvet heat into her mouth. His deep groan of pleasure filled her deepest recesses. When he reached for her breasts and rubbed the nipples in circular motions, she felt a fresh outpouring of need between her thighs—need that insisted on this man, the one with the power to possess her as no other man ever had.

She traced his length with her tongue, sucked the corded vein on the underside, then delved for his testicles, full and tight in their nest. She tickled them with her tongue and heard his soft hiss of indrawn breath. Slowly, lovingly she dragged her mouth up his length as if she licked dripping juice from a popsicle before she slid the tip back into her mouth and sucked gently.

When he pulled out, she gave him a questioning look.

"Too one-sided," he said. "I'm not so selfish."

He unsnapped her jeans and had her out of them in a thrice.

"I thought you'd like it," she said with a pout.

"I like it very much. But I'd rather be tasting you."

At his urging, she leaned back onto the seat across from him, open, waiting, ready to give and to receive.

It's all right to need a man, she told herself. At least for this.

He pressed his hand between her thighs. "You're so hot."

"You make me hot." This surge of desire that spilled through her threatened to drown her, but she was confident Brand would never let her drown. Never let her down.

He dipped a finger inside, outlining the shell-like contours of her woman's shape. "And wet. Has anyone ever made you this wet?"

Her eyes swallowed by his; she slowly shook her head from side to side. She could feel the sensual shift of her hair as it slid across her shoulders, following the sensual stroking rhythm of Brand's finger.

She was one limitless erogenous zone, riding a roller

coaster to the summit, fighting for breath. When he replaced his finger with his mouth and tongued the gently pulsing tip of her clit, she spun dizzily out of control, into a freefall complete with fireworks.

She'd barely recovered enough to begin the next climb when he stood and raised her legs so they wrapped around his hips. His cock pulsed against her opening, and she whimpered as she locked her ankles behind him and arched her hips invitingly.

As he entered her in one smooth stroke, the coach threw them together with an intensity that took her breath away. Paris wondered if a person could die from such ecstasy.

He held her legs to steady her as he continued to rhythmically plunge in and out. She watched, fascinated, as he pulled nearly all the way out and exposed the deep pink shaft that glistened with the mingled juices of their desire. His tip dragged deliberately across her clit to heighten the friction and intensity as he once more claimed her. His legs were like powerful columns, muscles tensed as he embedded himself inside her so deep she felt they had become one.

Yet she needed more. Needed it all.

"Faster," she said, panting, feeling her insides quickening in anticipation.

"Like this?" He increased the pace to a blur of motion, slick and slippery and deep, and as all of her swallowed all of him, she still craved more. They swayed together as the coach jostled from side to side and increased the tumultuous joining.

She kept her gaze locked on his, determined to see the expression on his face when he finally surrendered to the ultimate release. She squeezed him tighter with her inner muscles and watched him strain for control.

He'd always want control. And he took control now as he reached between them and found her engorged pearl with his talented fingers. It was all she needed to take her from the summit of anticipation into the throes of ecstasy. Her one coherent thought was that she was determined to take him with her. And she did!

Slowly she swam back to the surface of reality. Brand was splayed across her on the seat. Beneath them, the coach had stopped moving.

She poked him, pleased to receive a slight grunt in response. "We're not moving."

He rose enough to peer out the window.

"That's because we're here."

"Already?" Paris squeaked, fumbling for her jeans.

He pressed a hot, open kiss to her lips and she shivered at the taste of herself on his lips. "That was quite the ride. It's difficult to achieve the same results in the saddle."

"Difficult but not impossible?" Paris asked provocatively.

"Might be worth checking out one of these days."

Paris clasped Brand's hand as she climbed down from the coach on slightly unsteady legs.

The faint pink streaks in the sky to the east heralded the start of a new day. Forked Creek was still asleep, quiet as an abandoned movie set.

Brand knew something was wrong the second he set foot inside the hotel. He was relieved to find his instincts hadn't entirely let him down this time, or been clouded by the after-glow of sex that still hummed through his veins.

Barnes and Roper stepped in front of them and smoothly ushered them back into the street.

"I wouldn't go up to your room right now," Barnes said.

"Gotcha," Brand said. He turned to Paris. "The Wagon Wheel Café should be open by now. Let's go get ourselves some breakfast."

Chapter Twelve

Brand caught the way Paris glared at him across the scarred wooden table of the café. He'd guess she was more scared than angry, and this was her way of dealing with it. Anger was far easier to express and dish out, and he knew better than to take it personally.

He ordered them the gold miner's platter with ham, eggs, silver dollar pancakes, toast, and potatoes. It took more than a few dirty looks to ruin his afterglow.

Once the food was set before them, he dug in with gusto. Paris might be a little more amenable after she had something in her stomach.

"Don't you feel you owe me some sort of explanation?" she finally asked, her words frosty enough to chill a beer glass.

Brand wiped his mouth and dropped his napkin onto his empty plate. "About what?"

"Who those men were, for starters. And why we couldn't go up to your hotel room."

"Doesn't matter who the men are."

"I saw them get off the stagecoach the other day. They look mean."

Brand shrugged. "They can be. If the situation warrants it."

"And just what is this alleged situation?" Her voice started to rise and Brand gestured to her to keep it down. He took a quick look around the nearly deserted café, but the few other patrons didn't seem to be paying them any mind.

"They have ways of knowing things. If they tell me to stay out of my room for a bit, I know enough to listen."

"What's happening in your room?"

"I'd guess that it's in the process of being tossed by someone looking for the journal. Once they determine it's not there, they'll leave us alone."

Paris sighed in exasperation. "I don't understand any of this. What's so special about Martha May's journal that everyone's dying to get their hands on it?"

"Apparently whatever you find once you decipher the map could be of interest to other parties."

"I don't even know what I'm looking for. How am I supposed to know when we find it?"

Brand shrugged. "Instinct, maybe." He rose and dropped some money onto the table. "Come on. Let's go watch the moving pictures."

Paris dug in her heels. "You want to go to the movies right now?"

"Humor me," Brand said, pulling her reluctantly to her feet. "It's time I took you on a proper date."

They'd barely set foot out on the wooden sidewalk when they were greeted by Warren West.

"Morning, Brand. Miss Sommer." Warren tipped his hat in Paris's direction. "You're up and about early."

"Miss Sommer did me the pleasure of keeping me company over breakfast," Brand said.

"Where are you off to now?" Warren fell into step with them as if they were all old friends.

"Thought we'd go check out the moving pictures. Original old footage and all—I thought it would amuse Paris."

"Really?" Warren turned to Paris. "I understood you were here researching Martha May's time. Moving pictures weren't invented until years after she'd left Forked Creek."

Brand was gratified to see the way Paris moved a half step closer to him. "Brand has convinced me I should take in all Forked Creek has to offer while I'm here."

"Indeed? I had no idea Brand was such an ambassador for our humble town."

"There's all sorts of things you don't know about me."

"No doubt." Warren directed his attention to Paris. "Would you excuse us for a moment, Miss Sommer? I need a word in private with Brand."

Brand put his arm around Paris and drew her close. "There's nothing you need to say to me that can't be said in front of Paris."

"I just wondered about the status of that little project you and I had consulted on."

"Everything's coming together. You know these things take time."

"It appears time is one of those things that's in short commodity these days, given the determination of certain other parties. Any ETA?"

Brand looked at his watch. "Paris and I are on our way to the movie theater, as I said. Shall we get together early this evening?"

"That's an excellent idea. Why don't you join Mother and me for dinner at the house?"

"And risk her putting hemlock in my meal? I don't think so."

"She's mellowed, Brand."

"I'm fussy who I break bread with. Don't worry, I'll catch up with you this evening. Now if you'll excuse us, Paris and I have a date."

Brand was conscious of the way Warren watched them all the way down the next block till they reached the Grand Marquis.

"Do you think he was the one snooping in your room?" Paris asked.

"Warren would never lower himself to do anything that might soil his hands. He much prefers to delegate."

"Why is there no one here?" Paris asked as they went

through the empty lobby and into the darkened theater lit only by the flicker of black and white movement on the screen.

"The theater's open twenty-four hours, free of charge. The films play continuously."

"So there's no popcorn?"

"You didn't eat all your breakfast."

"I was mad at you."

Brand decided to play dumb. "Why would you be mad at me? Didn't I just make you come, oh, maybe . . . twenty times?"

"I lost count," Paris said, sinking sulkily into the old-fashioned double theater seat.

Brand chuckled and scooted closer to her. "Maybe we ought to start over. And keep better score this time."

She pushed him away, but not forcefully enough to really mean it.

"I'm still miffed. I've told you everything. I've shared the map and all my thoughts, yet you haven't shared a single solitary thing. Not why you're here. Who those men are. Or why there's all that tension between you and Mr. West."

How much did Paris need to know, and how much did she need to be told in order to trust him fully?

"Warren and I go back a ways. The men are unimportant. And is it such a stretch to think I'm with you because I enjoy your company?"

"I'm not stupid. I know there's a lot more to it than that."

"The long and the short of it is, there's more than a few

people in this town with an extraordinary interest in getting hold of whatever Martha May tucked safely away all those years ago. It's important that we get there first."

"Important to whom?"

"Once we know what everyone's so het up about, we'll be able to determine the players."

"So what are we doing sitting here? Let's get on with it."

Brand gestured to the screen in front of them. "It's like making a movie. It's all in the timing."

Paris folded her arms over her chest in a gesture of protection. Smart woman. She'd do well to protect herself from him.

"Time's running out, as far as I can see."

When she started to stand to walk out, Brand grabbed her wrist and linked his fingers through hers. Her face registered her shock as she plunked back down next to him.

"Paris, I know you're used to doing everything on your own. It's okay to accept help once in a while. Accepting help doesn't make you a weak person. Sometimes it makes you a smart person."

"I don't see you as easily accepting help."

He turned her hand over in his and traced the lifeline dissecting her palm, aware of the way her entire body responded to his touch, well aware of the way he could exploit that response.

"We're all vulnerable in one way or another."

"Even you?"

"Much as I hate to admit it, yes. Even me."

She pulled her hand away. "I don't believe it."

He reclaimed her hand and pressed it to his chest to let her feel the deep, regular rhythm of his heart. "Believe it, Paris."

He leaned forward and kissed her, only slightly ashamed of the way he was manipulating her. Better she be with him than charging off by herself on her treasure hunt, stirring up all sorts of vipers. He was just keeping her safe. He owed her that.

He felt her token attempt at resistance to his touch. Little did she know it was a wasted effort, for he always got what he set out after. Her lips trembled slightly, softened, then gave over. He felt a rush of triumph, a surge of primitive masculine pride, of mastery. After which he was instantly ashamed. Paris was a person with genuine feelings and emotions, emotions he was freely messing with. Sooner or later there was bound to be a fallout—but he'd worry about that later. For now, as she shifted in her seat and pressed herself closer, she belonged to him.

Ironic the way he, who never wanted to burden himself with possessions, found himself deep in the throes of the ultimate possession. For whether she knew it or not, Paris was half in love with him, a fact he intended to take full advantage of.

Right now she was breathing hard, cute little hiccuplike pants. "Relax," he whispered into her shell-like ear. "Let me kiss you. Just enjoy." He felt the tension slowly ebb from her as he feathered kisses across her parted lips, followed the hollow of her cheek to the contour of her cheekbone, then down to explore the curve of her chin.

Next her throat received his attention, arched and giving, eagerly awaiting his ministrations. He heard the faint mewling noise she made far back in her throat and felt her pulse race as he tongued the vein at the side of her neck. He followed it up the column of her throat to trace the shape of her ear, then alternately sucked and nibbled her lobe before once again settling against those delicious lips. He sipped delicately, and her sigh of pleasure filled him all the way to the farthest extremities.

Her impatience fueled his own desire, and the energy between them changed. Leisure turned to need and then to greed as he settled her on his lap, facing the screen. He could feel her heat coming at him in waves, bringing with it the musky smell of full female arousal. He unzipped her jeans and slid his seeking hand through the damp curls to find her essence.

She jerked as his fingertip slid across the slippery nubbin of her clit, to burrow deeper. She pushed off her jeans, then settled herself in the cradle of his thighs, her rounded tush enticingly pressed against where his cock strained against the zipper of *his* jeans.

His free hand opened her shirt and bra with a smooth, sure deftness. Her breasts landed in his palm as if they belonged there, hard, tight nipples begging for his touch.

He paid them their due, as his fingers traced her feminine petals inside and out, causing her inner muscles to tighten around his finger. Soon they would be tightening around him, gloving him, milking him. His cock responded with a jolt of hot pleasure and anticipation.

Soon, he promised himself. Right now it was all about Paris's pleasure. And did he have a surprise for her!

He moistened his baby finger with her dewlike desire, and ever so slowly, so as not to startle her, massaged the opening of her anus.

He heard her tiny gasp, her hesitation at this invasion, then felt the softening as her body reluctantly allowed him admittance. He deftly traded his finger for the magic lipstick tube he'd filched earlier from her bag, its hum inaudible over the film's music. As the toy vibrated against her and his fingers, he grew harder.

With a patience he barely knew he possessed, he stroked inside her front with his fingers, stimulating her anus with the vibrator, bringing her to a shattering release.

As she shuddered and sagged against him, he could feel the aftershocks ripple through her limbs.

He stood, supporting her, and skinned out of his jeans in record time.

Her eyes widened at the sight of his cock, swollen and plank straight, aimed her way, and her face softened with a secret, all-woman smile of anticipation.

Lightly, playfully, she pushed him back into his seat. Then she wriggled onto his lap, straddled him, and rubbed her hot pussy the length of his cock. Sweet torture and more as she guided the head to her clit and used it like her own personal dildo as she stimulated herself to renewed frenzy. She must have come at least two more times—warm-ups, really—before she took pity on both of them. Dramatically, she made a big show of lowering herself fully onto his shaft.

She had no mercy. Recklessly she used him for her own pleasure, riding him fast and furiously. Her thighs pumped as she raised and lowered herself a million miles a second.

Through the frantic motion he felt her come again. Slow and deep it started, gathering momentum as it rippled through her with it enough intensity to destroy everything in its path. Including him.

He let the sensation carry him right along with her, from this reality into the next. And as she collapsed, spent, against him, backgrounded by the grainy black-and-white image of a stagecoach bumping across the screen, Brand wondered what the heck passed for reality these days.

PARIS BLINKED IN THE BRIGHT SUNLIGHT as they left the movie theater, and felt Brand's arm steady her. She wondered if she looked as rumpled and sexed-out as she felt. Could passersby tell what they'd been up to moments earlier in the darkened confines? Moments earlier that felt more like a dream than reality.

What on earth had come over her, behaving in such a fashion? It was totally out of character. Yet wasn't that why she'd come to Forked Creek, to step outside of her comfort zone? She felt like Dorothy in *The Wizard of Oz,* waking up someplace unfamiliar after the tornado. Except instead of trying to find her way back home, she was attempting to find her true self. Not the person she thought her grandparents or friends or boss wanted her to be and expected her to act like. Her true self.

Was Brand a help or a hindrance in her quest? Could

something that felt so good possibly be right for her? Especially when it felt as if someone other than herself was now in control of her every thought, her every action. This had to stop. Unless this *was* her own true self? The person she'd come here looking to discover? How would she ever know, as long as she was with Brand?

"Brand, I think we ought to split up. We can cover more ground that way."

He braked to an abrupt stop and pivoted to face her. Somehow he managed to turn her inside out in a single look, without saying a word.

"I mean," she continued on in a rush, "this is hardly your problem. You can't even go into your hotel room when you feel like it, all because some hoodlum is up there. Because of me. Because of the journal, actually—"

"Stop it," he said harshly. "You don't mean what you're saying," he continued in a more reasonable tone. "You're scared; people often say things they don't mean when they're frightened."

"Those men don't frighten me, whoever they are."

"No," Brand said. "Right now you're far more scared by your feelings. The intensity of you and me together. That's why you want us to go our separate ways."

Paris clasped her elbows with her opposite hands and hugged. Was she really so transparent? "I guess you've done this so often that you know the routine by heart, then?"

Brand shook his head. "It's new for me as well. But I don't run in the face of fear. I meet it straight on."

Paris straightened her shoulders and held her head high.

She could be every bit as brave as he. "You scare the bejee-bers out of me, Mitchell Brand."

"Much better," he said as he flung an arm around her shoulders. "That we can deal with."

Brand's hotel room had indeed been "tossed." Paris found her bag emptied, its contents strewn across the room. The same with Brand's saddlebags.

"Messy, whoever they are," Paris said as she stooped to gather up her things.

"And they obviously don't care that we know they were here. Pretty amateurish," he said. "Why don't you grab the first shower while I clean up."

Paris didn't need a second invitation. She was dying for a shower, and even though it meant that she'd wash the smell of Brand from her body, she knew she'd never eradicate him from her mind. As she stood beneath the pounding hot water, she recalled their first shower, the intensity of that very first physical encounter. She'd never known anyone like him, and never would again.

She didn't know whether to be disappointed or relieved when Brand didn't join her. Typical man—the sex was done for now, so he was onto something new. Or had he intu-itively known that she needed this time on her own, to think about all that had happened? It was probably for the best, she told herself as she toweled her hair vigorously. She'd let him distract her completely. Good thing he was more fo-cused.

After her shower, she found him more than focused; he was downright enthused.

"Take a look at this." He handed her a piece of paper as he went past her to the shower.

He must have taken the shortest shower in history; clearly there had been no lingering, lost in fond memories of the two of them in there together, because he was back at her side before she'd done more than frown at his sketch. His handwriting was appalling, and his drawing even worse.

"You see it?" He was grinning from ear to ear.

"It's a map of the town." What was the big deal?

"What else?"

As he dressed with quick, economical movements, it was impossible not to admire the way the gas firelight played across the muscles in his chest and shoulders, the power and strength he exuded, his ease of movement. She gave a female sigh of appreciation as she returned her attention to his map.

Brand was saying, "Here's the town in the center. The clues from your word map indicate these key points on the outskirts. See?" She followed his finger and felt herself getting excited as she understood his logic. "Here's the mine. The hot springs. The bordello. The church and the cemetery."

"You've drawn a line through the town, from each point."

"Exactly. They all intersect at the apothecary, which could well be your final clue: 'Renewal of Life.' And one thing I know that you don't is that there's a network of tunnels under the town from end to end."

"Maybe that's where the treasure is hidden, below the apothecary!"

"Or in the apothecary."

"You're planning to just saunter in and ask the owner if he's happened to have come across something, Lord knows what, hidden there from the 1860s?"

By the look on his face, he was about to tell her something she wasn't going to be happy to hear. "Why do I suddenly get the feeling that you know exactly what Martha May hid for safekeeping?"

"It's just speculation—but there was a fire in the records office back in the fifties, when the town was still undergoing restoration. It was believed that the ownership deed to the bordello was destroyed in the fire, so the developer followed orders and included the bordello as part of the restoration."

"So?"

"So the bordello isn't officially inside the city limits."

"What does that mean?"

"That it's not protected by the same incorporation act as the rest of Forked Creek. Now Warren has applied to have it incorporated inside the city, since it's an important part of the town's history and needs to be preserved."

"And . . . ?"

"If the ownership deed falls into the wrong hands— Lamoy and his nasty cohorts have expressed a pretty keen interest—then the entire town is in danger of being compromised. There's no saying what kind of operation they'd be running out of there."

"Especially since they're already taping people in the rooms." She paused and studied him suspiciously. "And you, the mysterious outsider, have just managed to glean all this from saloon chitchat?"

"Paris, can we do this later? I'm anxious to check out the apothecary—I doubt Luke is far behind on the trail."

"No, it's time you came clean with me. Just for a change."

He sighed impatiently. "I lived nearby for a few years when I was a kid. Then my father died and I went off to military school. The day I left, I swore I'd never come back."

"So why did you?"

"Damned if I know. Coming to terms with some stuff from my past, maybe. Now can we go?"

She paused. "Do you think that's why Warren West was so unenthused about my presence? Maybe he thinks that I'm here, as kin to Martha May, to put a claim on the bordello property?"

Chapter Thirteen

"*No, Paris, I don't think Warren* thinks about things to such an extent." Warren's mother, on the other hand, was a devious old cow and might have reached that conclusion.

He hustled Paris into the late-morning hubbub of Forked Creek, weaving impatiently through the crowded wooden sidewalks.

"You don't think you and I might be related in some distant-relative kinky kind of way, do you?"

Brand stopped so abruptly, she bumped into him. "*What did you just say?*"

"I asked if there's any chance you and I are related."

Where in hell had *that* come from? "There's absolutely no connection between the Brands and Martha May."

"You're certain?"

"Yes. If you'd ended up doing the wild thing with Warren you might have cause for concern. But not with me."

"I just know there's a whole lot more you're not telling me. Like why you're in such an all-fired hurry this second."

Because once he managed to get his hands on the deed he'd be free to leave? In all honesty, though, it wasn't the deed or Warren keeping him here—it was Paris. The home truth hit him like a jolt of electricity. He'd never let himself get involved with anyone before, so why here? Why now?

"I just don't trust Lamoy."

"But why do you even care?"

Her question caught him off guard. Why *did* he care? There was little love lost between him and Warren, and he'd fulfilled any leftover obligation there. He didn't feel any re-sponsibility to the town, either. Which only left Paris and his desire to help her unearth what everyone else in town was on the hunt for. Was he hoping to prove something to himself?

"I don't care," he said gruffly. "You want to just forget the whole thing?"

"Remember when you made me look in the mirror the other day? Well, it's your turn to take a good, hard look. You're not being honest, Brand. Not with me and certainly not with yourself."

Brand stalked ahead of her down the wooden sidewalk. He hated it when other people were right, when they held up the reflection of all his inadequacies. Which was precisely why he preferred to go it alone. Yet Paris followed him, a constant reminder that he was no longer alone.

The bell over the door of the apothecary was clearly on the fritz, for it didn't announce their arrival. Inside, the air was tinged with the interesting musty smell of years past, overlaid with the pungent scent of herbs.

Paris wrinkled her nose. "Is this still a functioning store?" she whispered, the way one would in a church or a library.

"These days it's more of a museum. They grind stuff in the mortar and pestle for effect only. They're not licensed for modern dispensing."

"They had some weird stuff back then." Paris poked a small, plastic-wrapped bundle of what appeared to be dried animal parts. "This isn't quite eye of newt, but almost."

"Ssshhh." Brand pulled her back behind some shelves, out of sight. For once Paris didn't question him, but simply followed his lead. He listened carefully to the murmured conversation at the back of the store between the proprietor and Luke Lamoy, not sure if his ultrakeen sense of hearing was a curse or a blessing.

He risked discovery briefly and peered out just in time to see money and goods exchange hands. His purchase complete, Luke left the shop without a backward glance.

Brand gave her a nudge. "Come on. I want to see where he goes."

"You don't care for the man, do you?"

Brand wouldn't like any man he saw buying ruffie, the date-rape drug, but he didn't tell that to Paris.

Lamoy never once looked back as he leisurely made his

way through town. At first Brand thought he was heading to the bordello, but Luke surprised him by taking a turn past the livery. A block farther, the street petered out to nothing and the town ended. Nothing lay ahead in that direction except the old mine.

Brand paused, torn in indecision. He wasn't about to drag Paris out there, yet he was reluctant to leave her on her own. In the moment that he hesitated, Lamoy disappeared. One minute Brand had him in his sights, the next minute the man was gone, as if he'd been a figment of Brand's imagination. There had to be a hidden entrance to the tunnels around here, for there was nowhere else he could have gone.

"Do you mind telling me what that was all about?" Paris asked when Brand started back to the center of town.

"The apothecary is some sort of a front," Brand said. "Which makes me wonder what else is going on behind the scenes, and just how deep Lamoy and his bosses have their hooks into the town."

"I can't imagine Martha May hiding anything in the apothecary that it wouldn't have been discovered years earlier."

"Okay, Miss Smartie. What's next?"

"I think we ought to go back to the portrait studio, and this time we should have our photo taken."

Brand cocked a look at Paris. Something about her was different, something he couldn't quite put his finger on. "You're suddenly feeling photogenic, are you?"

"No, I feel like me. The new me. All my life I've taken everything too seriously: studies, work, life. I came here on what I thought was a whim, but here I am, chasing around way too seriously. I don't want to be serious anymore. I want to have fun. And take home the memories."

"What about the map?"

"I think you were right in the first place, that it doesn't exist. It's just a game I made up, wanting the journal to be more than simply a diary, to have some deep, dark meaning from the past. But it's time I faced facts. Things don't work out a certain way just because I wish them to."

Brand saw a shadow of sadness in her eyes, but she took his hand and tugged him down the street toward the portrait studio. "Let's go."

There was an air of near desperation about her forced playfulness and he suspected she was trying to snow him. Which meant the second his guard was down, she'd be off and running, chasing the treasure on her own. He should never have told her about the tunnels, because knowing Paris, that's where she'd head first chance she got.

He'd simply have to humor her till he figured out what was going on. He preferred to know what enemy he was facing right up front, which was why the special forces hadn't been for him. Everyone involved, friend or foe, could suddenly become the enemy.

Paris could tell that Brand didn't swallow her story and she really didn't care, for she'd lived all her life under a veil of suspicion. Her grandparents, although they loved her, had a deeply ingrained habit of questioning her every move.

She knew they feared the same rebellious blood ran through her as her wild-child parents, though she insisted she felt no connection to her parents and had no desire to experiment with drugs. She had been a Goody Two-shoes, still a virgin when she left for college, attending Sunday mass and confession on a regular basis. Since they'd never fully believed in her, why should Brand?

J. R. Stewart, Photography, was as deserted as last time. The same thin, balding man appeared from behind the velvet curtain and seemed delighted to see them.

"Might I hope that you've changed your minds about sitting for your portrait?"

"All the lady's idea," Brand said shortly.

"A very good decision, if I may say so. What particular theme are we embracing today?"

"Theme?" Paris asked.

"Certainly. There's the dance-hall theme, the gambler theme, the outlaw or hired-gun theme, the respectable lord and lady of the manor theme. There are others—those are just some of the most popular."

Paris looked to Brand for help. "Anything grab you?"

"Sorry, Princess. This is your party. You're here for the memories, right?"

"I'm not used to so many choices—and all of them right."

Brand approached the photographer. "Listen, we're going to need a little time and creativity establishing our theme. It's getting close to noon. Why don't you take yourself a nice, long lunch break."

"It's highly irregular." But the man's eyes widened with interest as Brand pulled out a roll of bills and started to peel them off one at a time.

"I figure a sign on the door telling folks to come back later might cost you a bit of business. So here's for your trouble." He pressed the bills into the other man's hand. "That got it covered?"

"I would think so, yes. Of course." His head bobbed eagerly as he pocketed the cash.

"Take your time," Brand said as he followed the fellow to the door.

Paris heard the click of the lock being thrown. A grandfather clock ticked in the stillness of the studio as Brand turned back to face her.

"Do you always take control in such a high-handed way?" she asked.

"All I'm doing is playing along." He held aside the velvet curtain and ushered her into the back room, where she was faced with an overwhelming array. Racks of costumes, heaps of props, a player piano, a claw-foot tub, feather boas of all colors, rifles, hats, and lifesize plywood cutouts that you could stand behind and stick your head through all fought for space.

Paris plopped down onto a red velvet settee. "All these choices are overwhelming."

"Some people never learn to make a choice. They're only comfortable when their choices are being made by others."

"Seems like I always opted for the safe choice. Which is not very different from having no choice, or feeling like I had no choice. How about you?"

"I follow my instincts." He had his back to her and she heard him tinkering with the player piano.

"But you must weigh in other factors."

"Nope. Make a move and consequences be damned."

Paris gave a wistful sigh. "That sounds very free and spontaneous."

"Or irresponsible and self-serving. Depends how you look at it."

Paris started at the sound of music, then realized Brand had gotten the piano playing. She clapped her hands in delight, watching the keys and pedals move as if the instrument was being played by a ghost. The familiar refrain of "Jeannie with the Light Brown Hair" began, and she smiled when Brand sang it "Paris with the Light Brown Hair."

"I do believe this just became our song." He bowed low before her, then pulled her to her feet and into his arms.

She joined him willingly, caught up in the magic of their surroundings. Even her dancing abilities seemed to take on new polish with him as her partner.

But she had to stop thinking that way. "Partner" made it sound as if they were a team, destined to last longer than a dance, longer than a fling.

But what a truly amazing fling!

She followed his lead, as he twirled her around, then bent her back in a graceful arc, holding her by the fingertips of one hand. She felt feather light as he drew her back upright. And when he looked at her that certain way . . .

It was far too late to tell herself not to fall for Brand, for her heart had already made up its mind. From the first moment she'd seen him, so rugged and untamed, something in him had triggered something out of control within her.

Something she'd suppressed all these years till now, when it was too late.

She used to be good at holding back. A multitude of disappointments, culminating with her being jilted, had taught her not to give up all of herself.

"What's the matter?" Brand reeled her close to him.

She sighed. She'd already given Brand everything, every part of her. Perfect Paris had been forever banished, replaced by a version she liked so much better. As if finally her skin fit the way it was supposed to.

"Nothing." She smiled. "Everything is absolutely perfect—one for the memory banks. So thank you for that."

"Shucks, ma'am, it weren't nothin'."

As if on cue, the song ended.

Paris went to look at the costumes, and as she sorted through them, a soft whisper stirred the air. A second later a circle of rope settled around her, catching her arms at her sides.

Her gaze flew to where Brand stood with a possessive intensity in his eyes that rocked her to the very core. He had her. Now what was he going to do with her?

An irresistible naughty-boy grin appeared as he slowly reeled her toward him.

"You know what they say: Anything you lasso, you get to keep."

Her heart kicked into overdrive as he staked his claim. "Does that mean you get to keep me?"

"All to myself."

"To do anything you feel like with?"

"Any little thing I desire."

Now a scant breath apart, Paris could see herself reflected in the depth of his eyes. Could she be part of him the way he was already a part of her?

It's all a game, she reminded herself. Soon I'll return to my old apartment and my old life, and I'll wonder if any of this really happened.

But Brand's hands felt very real as he slipped the lasso up over her head, his touch gentle.

She wasn't sure if she whispered his name first or he whispered hers as they came together in longing and need.

He plunged his hands through her hair and bent her back slightly, then kissed her as if it were the first time—or the last time. She tilted her head to offer up the column of her throat like a delectable morsel on which he grazed his fill. Long, delicate sweeps of his tongue tasted and licked, plundered and devoured.

"Shall I dress for you? Be your fantasy?"

"Princess, you are so much more than my fantasy."

"How would you like me?"

His eyes told her "naked beneath me," but his mouth curved in indulgence and she let out a pent-up breath. He understood how important this was to her.

"Saloon girls are a dime a dozen," he said. "I need you to be my fancy lady."

Chapter Fourteen

Brand's words proved Paris's ultimate undoing, for she heard something in his voice that unlocked one final reserve. She couldn't let him know, though. He'd mistake her feelings for pity.

Obviously someone long ago had taught Brand that he was inferior, beneath the notice or interest of a "fancy lady."

She managed to stay composed as she gathered an armload of clothing and disappeared behind the screen in the far corner of the room. Transformation complete, she stepped back for an overall view in the old-fashioned cheval mirror. Its surface was slightly rippled, making her reflection softer than real life, yet her image startled even her. What stranger stared back at her, veiled eyes sparking with hunger, cheeks slightly flushed? A warm, slow glow of inner excitement spilled through her.

The long-sleeved, high-collared, pleated white blouse sported a cameo at the throat and the long, slim dove gray skirt barely hinted at the curves beneath. She had tucked her hair up under a saucy forest green hat, and its provocative veil made her seem mysterious and desirable yet unavailable. Her white gloves and the fox stole over her shoulder completed the high-class, to-the-manor-born image.

Stay aloof, she reminded herself. You're much too good for the likes of the hired help, even if you burn for him. Her stockings ended halfway up her thigh and prickles of awareness danced across the bare skin at the top of her legs, radiating upward in a deliciously naughty way.

She pressed a hand to her heart to still the flutter of anticipation and forced herself to take a long, calming breath. She was Lady Chatterley. In the other room loitered the forbidden object of her lust—the dangerous and untamed lover.

She rounded the screen, struck a pose, then blinked against the flash as the old-fashioned camera caught her image. Pace by measured pace she advanced, keenly aware of the way Brand watched her from behind the safety of the lens. Did the camera's eye reveal things she'd prefer to keep hidden? Did it penetrate her aloof facade to the inner child-woman, revealing the secret part of herself long hidden and longer denied?

When Brand straightened to face her, something about

his stance, his expression, told Paris she had no secrets from this man. Somehow he knew every deep, unfulfilled fantasy, and the time for denial was long past.

She cleared her throat, aware her voice shook as much from nervous tension as from desire. "Why are you looking at me that way?"

"Because you're perfect, Princess."

Before Paris knew how it happened, he'd picked her up and literally tossed her over his shoulder, then carried her to the velvet-tufted settee and posed her. "Sit prim," he said. "Knees together, hands clasped in your lap. That's it."

He stepped forward and adjusted the stole across her shoulder and bosom, his hand grazing her breast. He made it appear accidental, yet they both knew it was no accident. The subterfuge inflamed her further, and sitting still became an effort as Brand stepped back behind the camera and clicked away, issuing directions.

"Look over there. Secret smile. Lick your lips. Head back now. Wait." He returned to her side and proceeded to re-arrange her.

Hat discarded, hair mussed, fur askew, and blouse partly unbuttoned, he settled her into a reclining position before he returned to the camera. The whir of the shutter became the only sound Paris was aware of.

"Perfect!"

Then he was back before her, frowning in serious concentration. This time when he reached to rearrange her, his hands were roughly impatient and exciting. He had her sit with one leg bent, her skirt pushed back, legs and stockings exposed. She felt the hot brush of his fingers on her bare thigh and jumped as if burned. She trembled with want, alternately hot and cold, a jumble of feelings, caught between two worlds, one a play-act, one a reality.

The one thing she was sure of was that she belonged to Brand. She had become his, body and soul, subject to his every urge and whim.

He untucked her blouse, then reached inside and tumbled her breasts free. He kissed her, with nothing soft about his possession, yet when she reached for him, he moved back just out of arm's length.

"I'm not done with you yet."

She gave him a haughty look. "Perhaps I'm done with you."

He flashed a self-sure grin. "I don't think so, fancy lady."

"Then stop hiding behind the camera."

"I'm not hiding; I'm using it to get what I want."

"What is it that you want?"

"The real you, fully exposed as surely as this film. No more secrets. There is nothing you can keep hidden from me."

"What makes you think I have anything to hide?"

"All women have secrets."

"All women have desires. And I desire you."

"Consequences be damned?"

That was certainly true. Brand was like a forbidden sweet treat. Sugar to the diabetic. Something you know is not good for you, yet you crave it all the same, perhaps even more so because of the danger.

"Take your clothes off," she ordered imperially. "I want to look at what I'm getting."

He leveled her a long, searching look, one that didn't give Paris a clue whether they were still pretending or had suddenly made the switch to the infinitely more dangerous real thing.

He removed his hat and sent it sailing through the air to land on a straight-back chair. His vest hit the ground at his feet with a soft thud, followed by his shirt.

Paris sighed with pleasure. Would she never tire of looking at him? The deliciously honed sculpture of his shoulders and arms, the shadowy fan of dark hair across his chest and the intriguing way it ringed his navel and arrowed south to disappear into the waistband of his jeans.

He shucked his boots and slowly unfastened his jeans. She could see the flat plane of his abdomen where the jeans parted, the shadowy triangle of forbidden male. Then he moved to stand before her, straight and proud, every inch the untamed male of her fantasies.

She placed her hands just inside the jeans opening to trace the wedge of revealed skin, and cull his warmth.

"It's for you," he said. "All for you."

"And I want it all." She purred from her throat, her voice barely recognizable as her own while he stood above her, a proud chief, a powerful warlord, and the next-door bad boy all rolled into one.

She slipped her hands inside his jeans, slid them around to cup his backside, then pushed his jeans down. He kicked them aside.

"You like what you see?"

"Very much."

She drank in the long, strong columns of his muscular legs, the flat of his abdomen. And slightly lower, enticing her from its rooted nest of dark hair, his sleeping cock.

She frowned. "You're not much good to me in this condition."

"Let me assure you, it's only temporary."

As he spoke the beast stirred.

Eyes never leaving hers, Brand took hold of it then began proudly stroking himself. He lengthened and thickened, the sheath of skin sliding up and down the widening shaft and a single drop of moisture glistened on the head.

Her body responded in kind. She could feel herself opening up, damp with readiness and need as he knelt above her on the settee.

He pushed her skirt up around her waist, exposing her stocking-clad legs. As he eased them apart, the air was a cool whisper against her heated inner lips.

He stroked her with the same knowing touch he had used on himself, spreading her dampness, stoking the flames of her desire until she trembled. She ached for him. She *needed* him.

He knelt above her like a conquering hero admiring his conquest, and she raised her hips in open invitation.

He grabbed hold of her bent knees and clasped them to his sides as he took his time with his approach.

She was breathing heavily, her body open in desperate anticipation, vastly empty without him. His cock finally rooted between her legs, still in no hurry, and finally, impatiently, she grabbed him and guided him inside her.

Her deep, delighted moan at the initial plunge of his possession fueled his response. Hard and fast and satisfying, his rigid cock slid in and out of her, smooth and slick. Pressure built as his speed increased, and Paris reached around to fondle that sensitive spot at the base of his cock. Gently massaging his balls, she then stroked his behind, raked her fingernails lightly up and down his back, and pulled him in hard for her kiss. He plundered her mouth, keeping time with the rhythm of his penetration.

She felt the start of an orgasm and tightened her muscles around him. He increased his pace, just enough to push her over the edge, and he swallowed her scream of release.

She felt him start to pull out and tried to hold him, but he was too strong, too determined. Her empty body pulsed, missing his. He laved her breasts, atoning for his earlier neglect, then sucked her nipples deep into the heat of his mouth, sending lightning deep down inside her.

He licked and kissed his way down her stomach, then lower, to nibble the soft skin of her inner thighs from her stocking top to her tabernacle of delight.

Paris tensed with arousal, and when his tongue darted inside of her with quick, sure motions, she pressed herself more tightly to him, striving for much-needed release. Hips gyrating, she moved with him and against him as she used him shamelessly for her own pleasure. Wave after wave of orgasmic release crested through her, each one higher than the other. Just when she thought she had reached total saturation, he replaced his tongue with his hot, hungry cock.

Her insides, super-sensitized and super-stimulated, welcomed his possession. She felt him inside so deep, so full, touching her in places she'd never been touched before, that when his thrust met hers, she was transported to an ecstasy she'd never reached before.

PARIS WASN'T SURE HOW AND WHEN she had lost Brand, but it was someplace between the ultimate crescendo and the postcoital cuddle. As surely as he'd been one with her, suddenly he was as good as gone.

The door was locked, so the photographer couldn't have returned. She glanced around, trying to fathom the cause. On the walls, black-and-white photos from yesteryear provided no clue to the sudden change in Brand.

Trying to restore the lightness, Paris slanted him a haughty glance as he fastened his shirt and tucked it into his jeans. "Is this the way you treat your fancy lady, Cowboy?"

"Dress-up time is over, Princess. Stay at Val's till you hear from me, and pretend you have no idea your room's bugged. Hang with the other girls for a change. I'll be in touch."

Then he left, like one used to issuing orders and having them obeyed. Obviously he didn't know her any better than she knew him.

She hung up her fancy-lady clothes and donned her familiar jeans, then peered into the mirror, well aware she'd changed in a myriad of ways she never would have guessed. More than simply shedding the skin of the "Perfect Paris" she'd always tried to be, she'd discovered her spirit. And it felt good.

She studied the photos on the walls, more shots of the

girls from Martha May's along with several of Martha May herself.

"I do believe I've already found the treasure you lured me here in search of, Martha May," she said aloud, tracing the woman's half-smiling features with the tip of her finger. "My true inner self. Thank you for that. I'll never lose sight of who I am again."

The photographer smiled widely upon his return. "I trust your time here was satisfactory?"

Paris gave a jerky nod, though she was still confused by Brand's sudden defection. "Sorry to be a bother, but I need the film from your camera."

"My camera? Which one?"

She pointed. "That big old-fashioned one on the tripod."

He laughed indulgently. "Oh, there's no film in that, my dear. It's simply another prop. A little piece of history."

"So you can't actually take photos with it?"

"No, no. I use the latest equipment when I do sittings."

"I see."

Paris took one last look at the collection of photos adorning the walls but didn't see anything that might have sent Brand off and running. So it must have been her. Well, if he couldn't handle the new, improved, self-assured Paris, that was his loss.

BRAND GAVE QUICKSILVER HIS HEAD and trusted him to find his way through the hills to Smyth's camp. This time no welcoming bullet whizzed past his ear.

The old man's humble cabin was as neat and comfortably

appointed as it had been decades earlier, but the fire was cold and there was no hint as to where Smyth might have gone.

"Damn! You've got some explaining to do, old man. And I'm not leaving until I've heard the truth."

IT DIDN'T TAKE PARIS LONG to reach the hotel, her stride echoing her determination. Brand had some nerve, thinking he could just cowboy off in that high-handed way and expect her to sit around twiddling her thumbs till he decreed different. She marched into the lobby. First she'd collect her bag, then she'd go to The Outpost, grab the journal, and leave this place behind once and for all. She had no further reason to stay.

Bad enough she'd embarrassed herself on a wild-goose chase for a treasure that didn't exist. Worse, she'd made a total fool of herself over a man who *also* clearly didn't exist. He was nowhere near the man she'd first thought him: a man of principles, a man worth caring about, a man worth falling in love with.

It wasn't difficult to sweet-talk the clerk into giving her a key to Brand's room. But when she arrived upstairs, the door was standing open—and the man inside wasn't Brand.

Chapter Fifteen

"*Well, well. Paris Sommer.* I had the distinct feeling we were fated to meet again."

"Mr. West."

"Please call me Warren. After all, as I'm sure you've figured out, we're practically related."

"I just stopped by to collect my things." She flushed slightly. But why should it matter if this man knew she and Brand had been intimate?

"Surely you're not planning to leave us as well?"

"As well?"

"As usual, Brand wasted no time hightailing it out of town."

She lifted her chin. "Brand is his own man. He's certainly not accountable to me." Really, it was better this way. No messy, drawn-out good-byes. She'd known from the beginning that Brand was the quintessential "love 'em and leave 'em" type. So why did it hurt?

Warren watched her closely. "Check with the livery if you don't believe me. You'll find man and beast both gone. Brand has a long history of disappearing anytime things aren't going exactly his way."

"I'm sure that's his business."

"It's your business as well, if he's absconded with Martha May's journal."

Something in his tone sent off shrill warning bells in her head, but she kept her face impassive. "What journal?"

Warren rose. "Come, come, Paris. Don't feel you must protect him. Because Brand is most certainly not protecting you. In fact, he's left you totally exposed and extremely vulnerable."

Paris picked up her bag and zipped it closed. "I'm afraid I don't know what you're talking about."

"Then you'd best come with me. I've arranged a little sneak preview for us."

Paris hesitated. She didn't trust West, or the way he was looking at her as he continued.

"You've certainly no cause to trust me or anyone else connected to Forked Creek, especially in light of Brand's desertion, but I fear you'll have serious regrets if you don't humor me in this instance."

He was starting to unnerve her. "All right, then. Let's get this over with."

THE MOVING-PICTURE HOUSE brought back memories she'd rather forget as she followed Warren inside its dark, empty depths. After they settled into the middle row, Warren gave a subtle signal toward the projection room. Someone was up there, but Brand had told her the place was automated. Had someone been lurking in the shadows, the other day, watching her and Brand?

The black-and-white film before them abruptly ended in midscene and the screen was taken over by a different scene. Paris gasped in shock as the camera panned the hills guarding the hot springs, then zoomed in for a close-up on her and Brand. A very personal close-up.

She turned to Warren in horror.

"Where . . . ? How . . . ?"

"Brand has a copy of this tape in his possession, but my partner possesses the original. It would make quite interesting viewing on the internet or on a porn channel. But my partner is willing to barter in exchange for the journal."

The screen before them went black. Seconds later, the old-fashioned black-and-white moving picture reappeared as if the action had never been interrupted.

"Of course, if Brand has the journal, then you're in a precarious position, for you've nothing to barter with and my partner can be most unpredictable."

If all the bordello rooms had hidden cameras, Val must have a very interesting collection of blackmail tapes. A most lucrative little sideline indeed.

Warren rose and glanced lazily at his watch. "It's four o'clock. Take a few hours to decide how you'd like to proceed. We'll be in touch."

How she'd like to proceed was to wake up from this bad dream, which had turned into a nightmare.

Brand must have known they were being filmed at the hot springs, hence his comment in the photo studio about her being "exposed." He knew something was about to go down that she wouldn't like, so he'd disappeared for parts unknown. Chances were good he'd stopped at The Outpost to recover the journal on his way.

Paris couldn't envision herself handing the journal over to a stranger—not even in exchange for the revealing tape. That journal was *hers,* the one thing in her family background that really spoke to her, and she wasn't about to give it up.

But she could pretend to.

VAL'S PLACE WAS ABUZZ with chatter about the upcoming street dance that night. Girls ran up and down the hallway exchanging gowns, shoes, and accessories.

Paris blanched at the sight of Val sailing regally through the main floor, dispensing advice. If she was Warren's partner it was important she act as normal as possible. "Hi, Val. Is it all right if I look for something to read in the library?"

Val gave a distracted nod. "Of course. You're coming to

the dance tonight, aren't you? The whole town turns out for the July Fourth party."

"I wouldn't miss it for the world."

"Somehow I get the feeling that your visit to Forked Creek didn't bring you what you thought."

"There have been some unexpected situations," Paris said.

"Remember what they say. This is a place where anything can, and often does, happen."

"That certainly fits," Paris said with a touch of irony.

Inside the library, she browsed through the books until she found what she was looking for: a volume with a cover that closely resembled Martha May's journal. In dim light, no one would notice the difference. At least, not until she had that tape in her hand.

She doubted Brand would return to Forked Creek, but just in case, she wrote a brief note informing him she was leaving town early and sent it to the hotel by the brothel's errand boy. Then she went upstairs to plan her strategy for the evening ahead.

THE CAMPFIRE BRAND HAD STARTED outside Smyth's cabin did the trick. The old cowpoke wasted little time reading Brand's signal and returning to his cabin.

"You lied to me."

"Never did no such thing." Smyth spat a stream of tobacco juice on the ground.

"You never told me the truth. Same thing, in my book," Brand said.

"You were a hothead," Smyth said. "Never quite knew how you might react."

"So you let me believe I was a bastard. That my father never bothered to marry my mother."

Smyth shrugged. "Told you more than once he loved her more than life itself."

"Talk's cheap. Proof's better. Why was their wedding such a big secret?"

"Her daddy didn't approve of yours. She figured she'd bring him around once you were born, but the poor girl never got the chance. Then your daddy was afraid the old man might try to take you away, so he kept a tight lip."

"I should have been told. Their freaking wedding photo is on the wall of the studio in town."

"New guy must have found it in the files and put it up without knowing who anyone was."

"You stood up with them. What happened to their marriage certificate?"

"That I couldn't say."

"Not that it matters," Brand said. "It just would've been nice to have known sooner."

"What would have changed for you, Boyo? If you'd known?"

Brand dismissed the question with a shrug. Knowing that his father had loved his mother enough to marry her made him feel more kindly toward his father's memory. Maybe even enough to forgive him for marrying Elspeth and turning their lives into a travesty. Where would he be if his father hadn't married Elspeth? If his mother hadn't died bringing him into the world?

He gave his head a shake. The "what if" game was pointless. Things happen; it was best to focus on the here and now. And right now he was thinking he shouldn't have left Paris that way. There was no one in Forked Creek he could trust as far as he could throw them.

"You're looking mighty serious, my boy. That little lady mean more to you than you're letting on?"

"No way," Brand said a little too quickly. "She's hell-bent on looking after herself."

"Those are the most dangerous ones."

"Dangerous how?"

Smyth gave a rusty cackle. "Dangerous in a million different ways to Sunday." He whistled for his horse. "P'rhaps I'll mosey down and have a look-see with you."

Brand didn't hide his surprise. "You haven't been to town in forever."

Smyth shrugged. "Like you told me earlier, never say never."

The fireworks started just as they reached the outskirts of town. Quicksilver balked and shied as the sound, like a volley of gunshots, was followed by colored lights exploding into a fiery arc of twinkling color.

"What the hell is that?" Brand muttered.

"I'm thinking it must be July Fourth," Smyth said. "Tend to lose track of the days, myself."

Brand had never seen the town decked out the way it was

tonight. It seemed as if everyone and his dog was out and about, the sidewalks and streets packed full of bodies. How on earth was he supposed to find Paris in that melee? It took forever to reach Main Street, which was lit up like noontime with gas lanterns every few feet. Music filled the air, and people were kicking up their heels everywhere he looked.

"I'll never find her in this crowd."

Smyth shrugged. "Then no worries. Neither will anyone else."

"I'm just going to check at the hotel, in case she's there." Smyth gave a nod.

Brand hitched his horse to the post outside the hotel and started through the lobby, only to be summoned by the clerk.

"Mr. Brand. A young man delivered this note for you earlier today."

"Thanks." He unfolded the paper with a feeling of dread. The message was short and to the point: Paris had left town.

He ought to be relieved. After all, he hadn't signed up for this tour in the first place. They'd had a fun few days, and . . . Had she really walked away without finding her hidden treasure?

Had she really walked away from him?

Of course she had. She'd run—he tended to have that effect on people.

Brand stared down at the note in his hand. He'd never seen Paris's writing. What if she hadn't written this? Or what if she'd been grabbed up by Luke and his cohorts and forced to write it?

He managed a rueful smile as he returned to the craziness outside. Something was seriously wrong when Paris in captivity was a happier thought than the clear fact that she'd had enough of him and taken her leave. What the hell was the matter with his brain?

Smyth had wandered off while Brand was inside the hotel, but Brand wasn't worried about the old guy. He reminded himself he had no cause to be worried about Paris, either.

PARIS MADE A GENUINE EFFORT to join in the excitement of her fellow Seattleites, but she was too distracted. Alone in her room, she made a show of tucking the fake journal into her purse, just in case someone, somewhere in the house, was watching her.

It was eerie not knowing if she was being observed as she brushed her hair and put on a little makeup and perfume.

"Are you going dressed like that?" Val asked, clearly disapproving Paris's casual sundress.

"I've had enough make-believe," Paris said. "I'm comfortable being me."

She liked the sound of her declaration. Brand had not only shown her how to be simply her, he'd also taught her she was an okay person to be. Better than okay—and that wasn't something she'd let go of.

Val shrugged. "It's up to you. But I sense you've held yourself back from the full spirit of your adventure here with us."

"Chalk it up to my being reserved by nature," Paris said,

smiling inwardly. She used to be reserved, but not any longer.

She stared skyward as fireworks illuminated the way from the bordello to the center of town, where the girls split off into smaller groups. Paris found herself alone as she watched the full moon slowly make its appearance. The air was balmy, yet she had goose bumps on her arms and her heart was pounding a million miles a minute. Would her plan work? Could she successfully trade the tape for the book in her bag?

As the fireworks faded from the night sky, she heard old-fashioned fiddle music up ahead and drew closer to see people dancing in the street.

She felt a momentary pang. If things had been different— if perhaps she and Brand had met under other circumstances—maybe they'd be together now, dancing close, oblivious to anyone else. Just another couple in the crowd.

She spied the perfect vantage point from which to observe without being seen. A metal fire escape on the side of the hotel led to a secluded balcony that projected out above the band and the people dancing in front of the makeshift stage.

The view from the balcony was wonderful, with the deep purple of the mountains in the distance and the light and shadows of the town's lanterns below, all watched over by a full yellow moon. The air resounded with people having a good time, and Paris leaned over the rail and drank it all in.

The pulse of the music throbbed through the wooden balcony and up through her legs, begging her to keep time. So intent was she on the music, the energy and rhythm of the night, it took her a while to realize she was no longer alone.

She knew it was Brand before he spoke.

"I thought you left," he said.

He moved to stand flush behind her, his arms loosely around her middle, his body cradling hers as he joined her in keeping time with the music. As before when they'd danced together, she melted against him. He felt so good, so right. Not two halves, but two wholes who joined forces to create an incomparable, complete unit.

"I was led to believe *you* had left."

He nuzzled the sensitive skin at the side of her neck. "I couldn't leave you."

Paris tipped her head back and drank in the velvet night sky. Had the stars ever looked so bright? Had her world ever felt so right?

Nothing felt more right than the slow, knowing glide of Brand's hands over her breasts, accompanied by the beat of the music below them which vibrated through her feet and up her legs. She exhaled softly as she felt her desire for him rise anew.

And as his hands slid up the back of her bare legs to push her dress out of the way, she made no protest. She felt his rigid cock press against the softness of her behind, seeking her hidden warmth, and she reached behind her to unfasten his jeans. He needed no further encouragement. Her panties were slid down her legs, and she felt the cool night air tease her sensitive flesh. He rubbed his cock along her inner folds to dampen himself with her juices.

Below them, oblivious, the crowd danced in celebration, while high above, she and Brand ignited their own private celebration. As she gripped the rail, and angled her hips, he entered her in one well-executed move that took her breath away. She held on tight and concentrated on the a harsh rise and fall of his breath, which kept perfect time to his cock's smooth possession and withdrawal. The music rose up, engulfing her, as Brand owned her. Together they moved, creating their own rhythm, performing their own timeless dance of the ages. A dance Paris knew she would never forget.

The music ended in a crescendo, followed by a flurry of applause from the audience. At the same time, Paris felt her body's crescendo of release, just as Brand's hot sperm spurted into her, propelling her to a whole new level of ecstasy.

They clung together as one, then slowly separated from the magic of their joining. Paris stepped back into her panties and smoothed down the hem of her dress, while Brand rezipped himself.

She turned to face him, clasped his head in her hands, and kissed him—a bittersweet kiss that acknowledged their time here was coming to an end.

Brand responded in kind. Each would leave with no regrets, no lingering good-byes, clean and neat.

He left first, and Paris left a few minutes later, thinking about the challenge ahead. Warren had said someone would seek her out.

She walked closer to the dancers and saw Val dancing with Warren. How comfortable they looked with each other. Could they be partners in crime as well as in dance?

Hayley and several of the others from her tour had found dance partners, and Paris envied their carefree frolics as she gripped her purse closer to her side and scanned the faces of everyone who came her way. She wished Warren's partner would approach her and get things over with.

She felt someone tap her on the shoulder from behind, and she froze, then whirled around. Was this her contact?

The older man doffed his hat and bowed low. "I'd be delighted if you'd do me the honor of accompanying me in the next dance."

Paris hesitated. Val's father—did he know what sort of place his daughter was running—that she was blackmailing her guests with taped sexual encounters? Or was he the "someone" Warren had said would be in touch?

Luke took her hesitation for acquiescence, for as the next song started, he two-stepped her into the center of the street amid the other dancers. As her partner whirled her around, she lost her footing and stumbled. The purse flew from her hands and skittered across the dirt road.

She raced after it, only to find it caught in the leathery hands of the old cowboy she'd met out in the hills with Brand. He gave a rusty grimace that might have been a seldom-used smile.

"Thought I might have to cut in on ya to get ya away from that snake oil salesman, but I'm too old for this dancing nonsense." As he handed her back her purse, she got the definite feeling he knew exactly what was in it.

"This way."

Once again, Paris hesitated. Warren hadn't said who his partner was; she had simply assumed it was Val. Could it be this grizzled old cowboy in front of her?

"Where are we going?"

"Someplace quiet. You and me have a fair bit to talk about."

Her eyes flitted over the people before she shouldered her purse, aware of being truly on her own. "Let's go."

So this was it, then. He was the one.

As she followed his bowlegged stride, it occurred to her she could be walking into a trap. On the other hand, he'd had her purse in hand and could easily have fled with it if that was his intention.

"Holy ground?" she asked, once it became obvious he was heading toward the church.

"Seems only fitting." The door hinges squeaked slightly as her companion opened it. Inside, shadows jumped and flickered as the candle flames fluttered in the breeze; the only other source of light was a dim glow behind the altar.

It was eerily quiet inside, and their footsteps echoed on the wooden-planked center aisle.

Paris could only hope the old guy's eyesight was faded enough that he wouldn't realize that he'd been duped until it was too late.

He didn't speak till they were up front, near the altar. "You're probably wondering what's so important that I dragged you away from the party."

"Oh, I've got a pretty good idea what this is about."

His eyes were unexpectedly keen and bright. "I doubt that. I figured it was high time somebody filled you in on exactly what all the fuss has been about."

"Smyth—what do you think you're doing?"

They both turned to the back of the church. In the open doorway, Brand's familiar form was silhouetted against the full moon.

Ridiculously, Paris was grateful for his presence. She'd told herself she could do this alone, but it was a relief that she didn't have to. Unless . . . Surely *Brand* hadn't arranged to have them taped at the hot springs? Surely he wasn't Warren West's partner in all this?

"I'm telling the little lady what she has a right to know, is what I'm doing."

Paris's heart fluttered madly against her ribs. Did she even want to hear what the old guy had to say?

Chapter Sixteen

"Smyth, you've spent a lifetime minding your own business," said Brand. "Why the sudden change?"

"Maybe I'm tired of sitting back watching folks make a hash of things that ought to be simple."

Paris's gaze swung from Smyth to Brand and back to Smyth. "You don't have the tape?"

His puzzlement was genuine. "Tape? I'm talking about the house."

"The house?" It was Paris's turn to be totally lost.

"Martha May's house. It stands just outside of city limits.

If'n the deed for it falls into the wrong hands, it could be the end of everything Forked Creek stands for."

"Brand already explained that to me. What he didn't bother to explain is just how someone managed to tape us out at the hot springs. You knew we were there. Was it you?"

"Save it, Paris," said Brand. "Smyth wouldn't know a video camera if it bit him in the ass."

"You knew about the tape, yet you deliberately kept me in the dark," said Paris.

"Who told you?"

"Your friend Warren West was thoughtful enough to arrange a private screening in the movie house. Up close and personal, if you grasp my meaning."

Brand looked taken aback. "I'm sorry you had to find out like that. I thought I had the only copy. I scooped it from Val's safe the same day I got the journal back."

"Just what's so important about the journal that it has everyone turned upside down over it?"

"Popular belief is that it holds the key to where the deed can be found."

"My gran was younger, but she was friends of Martha May," Smyth offered. "Said as how Martha were no fool. Always thinking ahead, that one."

"So why did she leave Forked Creek? Does anyone know where she went?"

"Gran said Martha left to go have her babe someplace private. Figured to maybe leave it with some nice couple, do the right thing by the baby."

"But she never returned to Forked Creek. Could she have

died in childbirth?" Paris hated to ask, but it would explain the absence of any later journal entries.

"Nothing of the sort. Gran got a letter a time or two afterward. Seems Martha May discovered she had maternal instincts she hadn't expected. She couldn't give the little gaffer up, so she went legit, even got married. Apparently she always intended to come back to Forked Creek one day and do something with the house. Just never got around to it, immersed in her new life and all."

Paris could relate to that. Immersed as she was in brand-new self-discovery, Seattle seemed like a distant past that faded with each moment.

"Was Martha May happy?" she asked Smyth, wanting so badly to hear it was so, that a person could totally alter her life for the better and have no regrets.

"'Course she was," Smyth said kindly.

"Thank you," Paris said. "Not only for telling me that, but for setting the record straight." She leveled a hard look at Brand. "So who has the original tape?"

"That would be me, my dear. Did you bring the journal?" The white-haired little old lady who joined them near the altar, leaning on her cane as she approached, didn't exactly fit Paris's idea of a blackmailer.

"How . . . ? Where did you come from?"

"Underground, I'll bet," Brand said. "Elsie knows all about the tunnels. She's probably the one who's kept them in such good repair."

"They have their uses—same as you, Brand. You make a wonderful scapegoat, much like your father." She turned back to Paris, who was so fascinated by the unfolding tableau she almost missed her cue.

"The journal," Elspeth snapped.

"In here." Paris tapped her purse.

"Not yet," Brand said.

Paris watched Brand's face darken with emotions he tried hard to keep in check. Certainly there were some interesting dynamics between the two, something she wasn't privy to—and never would be, she realized with a pang.

Brand and his problems weren't her concern. Making the exchange before anyone realized the switch she'd pulled was. Her hand trembled slightly on the clasp of her purse as she edged toward the baptismal font, feeling the need to put something solid between herself and Elspeth.

But the interaction between Brand and Elspeth was far from over.

"Why'd you marry my father, anyway? And don't tell me you loved him. You never loved anyone but yourself."

Elspeth's face darkened. "I had him first long before she bewitched him. No one walks away from me and gets away with it. Not until I'm done with them."

Brand nodded shortly. "Thanks for clarifying. It's a shame, the way you poison everything and everyone you come in contact with. But I knew this was too sophisticated a gig for Val to pull off."

"That silly girl is nothing without her daddy calling the shots. Same as my useless sop of a son. The two of them deserve each other."

Paris watched as her former dance partner, Val's father,

stepped out of the shadows on the other side of the old lady.

"Yes. A pity when everything is left up to our generation, isn't it? One gets quite tired of it after a time."

"Speak for yourself, Lucas. I'm never tired."

"No. You're actually quite proficient at hedging your bets, Elspeth. Allying yourself to all parties."

"I learned long ago where my loyalties lie."

Lucas laughed. "You trust no one. I daresay you don't even trust yourself."

"At least I know I have my own best interests at heart. That's more than I can say for the fickleness of the next generation."

"You're one of a kind, all right," Luke said admiringly. "That's why we make such a good team."

Paris wasn't the only one to hear a shuffling noise from the back of the church.

"Who's there?" Brand called. "Step forward and show yourself."

"Who put you in charge?" Warren stepped forward with a forced-looking swagger, Valerie at his heels. Dim candlelight illuminated his troubled features as the duo slowly made their way to join the others gathered around the baptismal font.

"At least I'm not hiding in the shadows, eavesdropping," Brand said. "Spying on unsuspecting victims for future blackmail. That's the coward's way."

"You've got it wrong, boy," Luke said with a laugh. "That's the effective way to get things done. Isn't that right, Elspeth? We're quite the team when we put our minds to it."

"Mother?" Warren said. "Did I hear right? You've allied yourself with the enemy?"

"Lucas and I are merely business partners."

"You know who his other partners are. And that they're hardly in keeping with the integrity of Forked Creek."

"Integrity," the old lady spat out. "Listen to your holier-than-thou tone—echoes of your father. I couldn't count on *you* to do things right."

"I should have known you'd sell us out. Me. Father. Grandfather. You have no interest in keeping their dreams and aspirations for the town alive."

"Pathetic and useless, the lot of you." The old lady spoke in such venomous tones that Paris flinched. "Takes a man who knows what he's doing to get things right. Lucas has the right kind of friends."

"The mob! Is that really what you want for Forked Creek?" Warren looked so shattered that Paris actually felt sorry for him, and was glad Val stood alongside him, gripping his arm in silent support.

"I want power!" exclaimed Elspeth. "I don't care where it comes from or who wields it, as long as I get my fair share."

"Then I wash my hands of you," Warren said.

The old lady let out a monstrous cackle. "You really are your father's son, aren't you? He tried the same thing. Look where it got him."

"I always wondered about that," Warren said thoughtfully. "Such a convenient hunting accident. A little too convenient, perhaps."

"Pah! You'll never prove a thing. It's all conjecture."

Paris gasped as Luke grabbed Warren and gave him a shake. "Sonny, that's no way to be talking to your mother. Now you go on over there and apologize."

"When hell freezes over," Warren said.

Sometimes, when she was growing up, Paris had thought it would be nice to have real parents like the other kids. But not the likes of what she saw here tonight.

Warren began to struggle in Luke's hold, and Brand moved toward them.

"Let him go, Luke."

"You man enough to make me?"

"You can't fight us both," Brand said mildly.

"The hell I can't."

"Leave him," Elspeth barked out. "Neither of them is worth the breath you're wasting."

Luke released Warren just as Elspeth leveled her gaze on Paris, who shuddered at the soullessness of the woman's gaze. Were some people simply born evil or did they slowly turn that way?

"Young lady, I want that journal and I want it now!"

Paris refused to be cowed. "In exchange for the tape. And I require proof that there are no more copies."

Elspeth raised her cane and brandished it as if it were a weapon. "Proof, my fanny. Luke, take the book from her."

"I don't think so." Brand stepped between Paris and Luke. "Not unless you go through me."

"And me." Warren stepped up next to Brand.

These two might think they were nothing to each other, Paris thought, yet they were each constantly stepping forward to back the other one up—a loyalty that meant more than all the blood ties in the world.

Luke heaved a mighty sigh. "I sure do hate doing things the hard way." Moving far more quickly than one would expect for a man of his age and girth, he secured Smyth in a choke hold in front of him and held a pistol at Smyth's head.

"Don't be giving in to the vermin," Smyth said. An ominous click echoed through the church as the safety clicked off.

"Daddy," Val said, her little-girl voice totally at odds with her mature appearance.

"Be a good girl and mind your own business, like I taught you. Miss Elspeth and I are tired of dancing around, as are our associates. Now hand over the book, missy."

Paris made a show of wrestling the book from her purse. She waved it through the air within plain sight of everyone there.

"It's only a book. It's not worth spilling blood over." She set it down on the edge of the baptismal font. "Now let Smyth go."

The second Luke reached for the book, Brand and Warren were on him. Fists and feet and bodies slammed into the baptismal font. The basin teetered and everyone leapt aside as the heavy stone crashed to the floor, along with the book.

Water sprayed everywhere, drenching the pages. The ink ran across the sodden mess, making the words illegible.

Elspeth stood shaking with rage. "You've ruined it. Buffoons, the lot of you!"

For once no one seemed able to say a word. Paris squatted

and attempted to retrieve the soggy mess but the hundred-plus-years-old book disintegrated. Thank God the real journal was safely locked away at The Outpost.

She straightened and faced the old lady. "I still want that tape. Hand it over."

"Never."

"I fulfilled my end of the bargain."

"Not until I have that property deed in my hand."

Warren stepped forward. "Over my dead body will you get control of that deed and destroy everything my father worked for, including this town."

She cast him a withering look. "If need be."

She turned and marched down the center aisle, back straight, head high, the thump of her cane measuring out her steps. She paused halfway. "Lucas, come along. We have our work cut out for us."

Paris let out the breath she had been holding as the church door closed behind the duo. Warren extended a hand to Brand. "I guess it's about time I said thanks for your support."

"Sorry not to be more effective."

"Can't say you didn't try." There was a strained silence, and Warren cleared his throat. "Maybe once things settle down, you might consider finding your way back here. I could always use someone I can trust in my court."

Brand took his proffered hand. "You never know. I tend to move around a fair bit."

"Anytime you feel like moving this way, you just let me know."

Brand nodded.

As Warren stepped next to Val and put a sheltering arm around her shoulder, he seemed far more capable and in control of things than before.

Smyth, too, prepared to take his leave. "Now you know why I stay away from townsfolk. Too hectic and crazy down here."

"What I said to Brand goes for you as well," Warren said. "There'll always be a place here for you."

The trio took their leave, which left Brand and Paris alone in the empty church. A weighty silence hung between them, and neither seemed to know where to look.

"Well, then. . . ." Paris's gaze flitted around the church. She couldn't look at him. Not when there was still so much to say, and no words for any of it.

His body language didn't help, for he'd adopted a defensive pose, arms folded across his chest. "For the record, I didn't know we were being taped that day. I was angry when I learned about it, and royally pissed at myself for not being more aware." He sighed. "You got to me and I let my guard down. That's never happened before. It shook me up."

She tried for a teasing smile. "I won't spread it around, if that's what's worrying you."

"I'm not worried. I'm . . ." He bit off his words. "I still can't believe you were prepared to turn the journal over to Elspeth. Not when I know how much it means to you."

Should she tell him the truth? How could she deceive him any more than she could deceive herself? It was hard enough to pretend she didn't love him.

"I promise you this," he went on. "I will get my hands on that tape . . . However many copies there are, I'll personally see that each and every last one of them is destroyed."

Paris nodded. "I trust you to do that."

He looked startled. "You trust me? After everything that happened here?"

"One thing I know is that you're a man of your word, Mitchell Brand."

"You're not holding it against me? The fact that the journal got destroyed?"

Paris's smile widened. "The real journal remains safely locked away at The Outpost, right where we left it."

"But . . ." He indicated the ruined pages on the wooden plank floor.

"That's a book I snagged from Val's study."

Brand laughed out loud.

Paris shrugged. "I wasn't about to hand over the real journal. Not when I didn't even know who I was dealing with."

Brand grabbed her and hugged her. "A woman after my own heart."

Paris froze in his embrace. This was no time to be holding out false hope, to search for meaning that didn't exist behind his words.

He must have felt her lack of response for he released her immediately and Paris felt as if everything inside her would wither and die from starvation. How unfair. Here she was, overflowing with love, and no one with whom to share any of it.

She gave a weighty sigh, and stepped closer to the base of

the baptismal font. "Do you want to try and lift this basin back into place?"

"I suppose we should."

As they approached it together, they both noticed something at the same time.

"The base is hollow," Paris said.

"There's something inside," Brand added.

They glanced at each other in hesitation. "Go ahead," Brand said. "Your hand is smaller than mine."

As Paris reached into the hollow crevice, her heart gave a ridiculous leap of hope. Could it be possible? Had she accidentally found Martha May's hiding place after all?

"Hope Springs Eternal. Renewal of Life," she quoted in wonderment.

"Untapped Riches. Cast-off Temptation," Brand added.

Could her word mapping have been right all along? Paris took a huge breath and reached inside, where her fingers found the brittle edges of paper. She pulled out a rolled document secured with a faded red ribbon.

Her hopes were instantly dashed. "This is far too modern to have any connection to Martha May."

"Check it out anyway."

Carefully she unrolled the intact document. "It looks like a certificate of marriage." She paused and gave Brand an intense look. "Mitchell Brand the second and Jessica Turner, June nineteenth, nineteen hundred and sixty-nine."

"I'll be damned." Brand reached for it. "Smyth told me they'd been married, but I had no proof. Until now."

"I gather this is important to you," Paris said.

Brand smoothed the edges of the certificate. "Maybe one day I'll explain to you just how much it means to me. Thank you for helping me find this, Paris."

The look in his eye drew her to him as effectively as steel to a magnet. And even when she was exactly where she longed to be, she was unprepared for the impact of his kiss.

It stole through her, invaded her, possessed her, became her. And still it wasn't enough.

It would never be enough.

She wound her arms around his neck, drinking in the way his lips knew hers with an intimacy that rippled through her entire body. She shared his breath, let it feed and nurture her. His hands roamed the length of her back, then cupped her bottom as he molded her body to his. "God, Paris, I . . ."

He tried to pull away but she followed him, denying his release, knowing even as she did so that he wasn't hers to keep hold of, and never would be.

When they finally broke apart, this time by mutual agreement, both were breathing heavily. Brand shoved a shaky hand through his hair and flashed her an endearing half grin. "I have the feeling we'd rot in hell if we were to take this any further. I know the altar used to be used for sacrifice in some religions . . ."

"What's this talk about sacrifice?"

Brand gave his head a quick shake. "I'm still off balance from finding that marriage certificate. I spent my entire life thinking my father hadn't loved my mother enough to do the right thing by her, believing he wasn't man enough to commit to the woman he loved."

He bit off his words abruptly.

Paris felt herself inwardly deflate.

"Paris, I . . ."

"Come on," she said abruptly. "Let's give this basin another try."

"Wait a sec." Brand stuffed his hand down inside the narrow hollow base. "I think there's something else in here. All the way inside, way to the bottom." His entire arm disappeared to the shoulder, yet he grimaced and came up empty-handed. "Can't quite reach." He glanced around. "No wire coat hangers in this place. What can I use?"

"How about this?" She approached the altar and picked up a heavy silver candlestick. She removed the candle and passed him the tapered holder.

"Worth a try." He took it and delved inside the hollow stone base. Sweat beaded his upper lip with the exertion. "Whatever it is, I've managed to pull it partway up on your side," he said. "It's flush against the wall. Your hands are smaller. See if you can get a hold of it."

Paris wedged her hand down inside, past the candlestick, till the tips of her fingers brushed something soft.

"I can't quite get it. Almost. Can you pry it up a little more?"

"I'll try."

She saw his muscles tense with the effort, his face straining in concentration. This time she managed to grasp a corner of a cloth-wrapped packet and pull it free.

"Let's see what we've got."

Paris carried the second bundle to the altar. As Brand replaced the candle in its holder, she unrolled the aged cloth. Inside was a fat envelope, yellowed with age.

"Go ahead," Brand said. "I have a feeling this one's for you."

Her hand shook as she pulled out the papers inside and saw handwriting that was achingly familiar.

"Martha May's will," she said in hushed tones. "Along with the deed to her house."

Together they read the faded handwriting.

Paris stifled a gasp and turned to Brand. "Do you think it's valid?"

"I don't know why it wouldn't be. It clearly states that she leaves all her worldly goods, including her house, to her offspring and their offspring in perpetuity. That sounds like you."

Chapter Seventeen

"That was some discovery," Brand said, as they made their way through the dark deserted streets to the bordello. It seemed a hundred years since they'd watched the music and dancing.

"Yes," Paris said. "Martha May probably had the priest help her stuff her will in there before she left town all those years ago."

"And a different priest must have hid my parents' certificate of marriage after the ceremony, knowing he could get to it anytime he needed to. Since my mother was under age, her father could have had it annulled, had he found out."

"Quite romantic," Paris said. "Your parents, I mean. Kind of Romeo and Juliet-ish."

"I wish I remembered her," Brand said. "All I know is what my dad told me, and all mention of her ended when he married Elspeth."

"Poor Warren," Paris said. "Imagine having her for a mother. She's some piece of work, all right."

"Paris, I—" Brand stopped abruptly. "What the heck?"

Around back of the bordello stood the tour bus with its lights on and the motor running. The house was ablaze with lights from every window. Paris and Brand quickened their pace when they saw the Seattle girls milling about between the house and the bus. Hayley broke into a smile and ran toward them.

"There you are, Paris. I was afraid we might have to leave without you."

"What's going on?"

"It's totally wild, like something from a reality TV show! Some special agents came and arrested Val and her father for extortion. The house is being sealed up for evidence. Apparently there're hidden cameras in all the rooms, and access to a bunch of tunnels down below the house. Totally 'out there'! They're busing all of us to someplace nearby called The Outpost before we head back to Seattle in the morning. I grabbed your stuff from your room for you. You sure do travel light."

On the front porch, Paris recognized one of the men who had stopped them from going into Brand's hotel room that day. She saw the look that flashed between the two and felt

Brand's instinctive withdrawal from her. Not that it mattered, when he had never been hers to start with.

"I have to go see someone," he said. "I'll catch up with you later."

She might be light of possessions, Paris thought as she watched Brand hurry to confer with his buddy, but her heart surely did feel heavy.

She was proud of herself for the way she climbed aboard the bus with the rest of the girls, not pausing to look back even once.

TRUE TO HER EXPECTATIONS, Paris didn't sleep a wink in the hotel her group had been escorted to. Eventually she gave up and made her way to the train station locker, knowing she'd feel better once she had the journal back in her possession. She twirled the combination lock, opened the door, and reached inside, only to find nothing except a folded sheet of paper.

She blinked and took a second look to be sure. Why would Brand have taken the journal? Even if they needed it for evidence, which she highly doubted, he ought to have checked with her first.

She unfolded the paper and found a short note:

Rainbows ahead in Emerald City.

What was that supposed to mean?

She puzzled over the message the entire bus trip back to Seattle. Once back in the city, her apartment felt closed up and stale, the city and traffic too loud and busy after the olden-days ambiance of Forked Creek. It didn't feel like home, she realized. In fact, it never had. It was simply some-place to live. And what kind of life was this?

As she looked through the flyers and junk mail, she found a hand-addressed envelope in familiar writing. Her hand shook as she tore it open.

You had the ruby slippers all along.

This meant even less to her than the first one. Perhaps Brand had overdosed on *The Wizard of Oz* as a child, for El-speth certainly was a wicked witch. Had the evil woman been caught in the clean-up by those special agents, or had she gotten off scot-free? Somehow Paris doubted Luke and Valerie would let that happen.

When a third note was delivered to her the next day at work, Paris finally realized that Brand was creating his own word puzzle for her to solve. Since she had no way to contact him, she could only wait and look forward to the arrival of each new clue.

C is for courage, which you have in abundance. It's also for change.

H is for heart and for home.

She caught her breath. It was almost as if he could see right into her mind and know she was discontent with her life.

Follow the yellow brick road. On the seventh day all will be re-vealed.

The handwritten clues continued to arrive, leaving Paris consumed with curiosity and impatient for Saturday.

The sixth and final clue saw her aboard the Bainbridge Island Ferry from downtown Seattle. She stood on the upper passenger deck and watched the cars drive onto the car deck below, wondering what on earth she was doing playing some hide-and-seek word game with a man she barely knew.

All she wanted was the journal back. What was he trying to prove, anyway? She had no time for his games and she couldn't wait to tell him that. If he dared show his face in her presence.

The ferry was loaded and set to depart when she heard the roar of a powerful motorcycle drive on board. Below her, the driver dismounted, removed his helmet and glanced upward, directly at her. Her heart caught in her throat. He was wearing modern-day chaps and he'd traded his horse for a Harley, but he was still her cowboy. The man with the power to turn her world upside down again and again and again.

In no time, he was walking toward her. He looked the same, yet different. The chaps were new, the Stetson was gone, but nothing could erase that devil-may-care, cocksure walk of his.

"Why the games?" she asked when he finally stood in front of her.

"I thought I owed you this week of your life. To settle back into the familiar, revisit the comfort zone and try it back on for size."

The comfort zone no longer fit. She'd been bored out of her mind. His daily note had been the one highlight she looked forward to, and he was the first thing she thought about in the morning and the last thing she thought about at night.

"Since you were so good at word maps, I figured you'd be equally good at figuring out my clues."

"Obviously I'm not, because I seem to be missing a big one. Why am I here? Why is either of us here?"

He pulled the journal from the inside pocket of his leather jacket. "For one thing, I had to return this to its rightful owner."

She reclaimed the book, which suddenly seemed less important than Brand. "You could have sent it by courier."

"True. But then I wouldn't get to see you."

"Did you want to see me?"

"Paris, I spent my life resenting my father because I thought he didn't do right by the woman he loved. It was a relief to find out different—and a shock to realize I had followed the exact same pattern in all my relationships. Not just with women, but with Warren, my bosses—everyone.

"It's a pattern I'm determined to change, starting here and now. I love you, Paris. I want whatever it is *you* want. If you want to live here, then it's where I live also. If you want to get married, we'll get married. If you want to live together and get to know each other first, that's fine by me. If you want to travel around in search of adventure, I'll be at your side. If you want to move to Forked Creek and look after your property, I'm there with you. Whatever you want, I will love you and support you and try to never let you down. Is that clear enough?"

Paris's eyes widened their widest.

"Well?" he prompted.

She blinked back her unshed tears. "All my life, all I ever wanted was for someone to love me, just the way I am."

"Loving you is easy, Paris. Think you can love me back? God knows I'm bossy and difficult."

Paris stepped confidently into his arms and smiled up at him. "I guess I'll have my work cut out for me, then, won't I?"

"And I guess we have forever to talk about the rest of our lives."

"One thing you should know," Paris said. "I saw my lawyer. I've started to make arrangements to turn the bordello into a museum, once the authorities have finished with it."

"What a great idea—I'm sure Martha May would approve."

"And I gave notice at the library."

"Really? Why's that?"

"It doesn't feel like a good fit anymore. I love books, and realized I don't want to simply shelve and catalog them. I want to publish them, to be part of the process between author and reader."

"Where would you do that?"

"Anyplace I want. But I must confess I'm partial to the Pacific Northwest."

"That's handy. Because one of the businesses I own happens to be a Christmas tree farm not far from here. There's acres of room to do whatever we want on the property."

"Where are we off to when the boat docks?"

"Wherever you want. For a day, a week, a month, a lifetime."

That was good enough for her. As Paris wound her arms around Brand's neck, she knew for sure this was another decision Martha May would applaud.

As they stood locked in an embrace on the deck of the ferry, it started to rain, a light, misty West Coast summer rain.

"Darn," Brand said, glancing at his watch.

"It's only a little summer rain," Paris said. "It'll blow over."

"I just hope it doesn't wreck my surprise."

She stayed secure in his arms until the ferry docked a short time later. Snugged up against Brand on the back of the Harley, they drove off first.

Paris blinked at the sight ahead, then laughed out loud. "The yellow brick road!"

"That was my surprise." The road leading off the ferry had been painted bright daffodil yellow, which was starting to wash away in the rain.

Paris nuzzled the back of Brand's neck, awash in a warm glow of total and utter happiness. "Truly, there's no place like home." And home would be anyplace she and Brand found themselves together.